Frankenstein's Hamster

Frankenstein's Hamster

Ten Spine-Tingling Tales

written and illustrated by Barbara Griffiths

DIAL BOOKS

New York

First published in the United States 1992 by Dial Books
A Division of Penguin Books USA Inc.
375 Hudson Street
New York, New York 10014

Published in Great Britain 1990 by ABC, All Books for Children
Copyright © 1990 by Barbara Griffiths
Design by Ann Finnell
All rights reserved
Printed in the U.S.A.
First Edition
3 5 7 9 10 8 6 4 2

Library of Congress Cataloging in Publication Data
Griffiths, Barbara.
Frankenstein's hamster : ten spine-tingling tales /
written and illustrated by Barbara Griffiths.
p. cm.
Summary: A collection of ten scary stories featuring
a schoolboy with a talent for taxidermy, the highwayman
of death, and other disturbing characters.
ISBN 0-8037-0952-8
1. Horror tales, English. 2. Children's stories, English.
[1. Horror stories. 2. Short stories.] I. Title.
PZ7.G88367Fr 1992 [Fic]—dc20 91-25912 CIP AC

For Tom and Edward

CONTENTS

Frankenstein's Hamster

Frankenstein's Hamster

The Story of How a Boy Makes a Friend

T hat is it, Luke. You've had your last chance. I will NOT have you talking to Steven during class. Take your book and come to the front, where I can keep an eye on you."

"But I only wanted to borrow his ruler!"

"That's enough. Sit here, next to Franklyn."

"Sorry, Mrs. Milne. Please, Mrs. Milne?"

"Now! And you will sit there till the end of the term. Continue reading, Franklyn dear."

Luke shuffled into the other half of Franklyn's desk. If there was one thing worse than being moved away from his best friend, worse than being moved to the front row, it was having to sit next to Franklyn Stone. Franklyn wore knee-length gray shorts and a V-necked pullover sweater with a tie. However, his mother's efforts to make him look like a bank manager were doomed—his nose was always running, leaving snail tracks across his sleeve, and his shirt hung out with the buttons in the wrong holes. When he was skulking by the toilets at break, wearing that creepy black duffel coat, he looked more like a child molester. And it wasn't just his appearance; instead of taking a healthy boyish interest in things like fast cars, computer games, and horror videos, he liked botany and science. They were studying geography now, and Franklyn was reading his essay.

"Grazing land is essential to the economy of Australia. Rabbits, introduced in the last century, have become a pest due to the fact that one rabbit can eat as much as seven sheep."

Luke imagined rabbits tiptoeing up behind flocks of sheep, pouncing, and savagely devouring them seven at a time. Funny how the most boring lessons sometimes came up with amazingly interesting facts. But math could never be anything but deadly. What sort of question was this: "If Janet has six feet and John has three, how much string do they need to make up twelve yards?" He was busy drawing a spider named Janet when he felt Franklyn breathing in his ear.

"Do you want me to help you, Luke?"

"I've done it in my head already. No sweat. Why, what did you get?"

"N-Nine yards."

"Well, what a coincidence, Franklyn. That's just what I got. Must be right," said Luke, scribbling in his book. History was also less painful sitting next to Franklyn. Take Joan of Arc, for instance. Was she Noah's wife, who got her bit of fame by burning the steak? Or was that King Alfred? Franklyn discreetly made all clear, and was rewarded after lunch when Luke picked him for his soccer team.

"Jeez, Luke, what did you ask Quasimodo for?" complained Steven. Franklyn's legs flailed enthusiastically as he circled the ball.

"Oh, well, it's only fair—they've got Gary the Gut," Luke apologized. He winced as Franklyn delivered the ball to their own goal, turned, and beamed. His arms were waving, his glasses flashed. Luke pretended not to see and walked back up the field. He heard Steven swearing behind him.

"Whadja do that for, chicken face? Crawl away, will ya?"

He heard flapping like a galleon in a gale as baggy-shorted Franklyn caught up with him.

"Sorry, Luke. I was just so excited, I got confused."

"How can someone who understands algebra not tell one goal from another?"

"I'm sorry, Luke. Really."

Mr. Perry blew the whistle. "Back to your positions!"

Soon Franklyn had the ball again and this time purposefully headed in the right direction. Luke jumped up and down, trying to attract his attention. Franklyn saw him. With great concentration he balanced on one leg and slowly drew the other back to kick the ball. At that moment, Gary was gathering all his strength and wobbling toward Franklyn. The teams watched in fascination as resistible force met moveable object at the speed of a slow motion instant replay.

When Gary rose triumphantly, Franklyn was still in the mud, flat as a gingerbread man. Mr. Perry hauled him up.

3

"Hey, like dem cool dark glasses, Frankie," called Steven.

The lenses were brown, and so were the rims and the pieces of adhesive tape holding them together. So was all of Franklyn.

"That's enough," said Mr. Perry. "Go and take a shower, twinkletoes."

Luke felt a twinge of pity as he watched the hunched figure limping up the field—every drooping, soggy line expressed misery. Then the whistle blew, and he gave way to the pleasures of the game.

An alliance developed between Luke and Franklyn. There was an unspoken rule that Franklyn shouldn't approach Luke at break, but in exchange for homework favors, Luke would teach him soccer once a week. Luke liked to kick a ball around after school, and sometimes he even felt fond of Franklyn, who galumphed up and down the field like a big dog. The doggy adoration was nice too, and the feeling of superiority it gave him.

One morning as the bell rang for lunch, Franklyn slid an envelope across the desk. As Luke tore it open, Franklyn ran off. There was a letter inside, on mauve paper.

> 54 Belladonna Avenue
> Friday

> Dear Luke,
> Franklyn and I would be delighted to have
> the pleasure of your company for an after-school
> snack next Thursday. I look forward to making

your acquaintance, as my son has told me SO
much about you.

Yours sincerely,
Mrs. Winifred P. Stone

Luke, embarrassed, thrust it deep into his desk. Was it some sort of joke, or what? He decided to ignore it. Anyway, Thursday was practically a week away. He went off to find Steven and forgot the letter.

Thursday afternoon arrived. As Luke swung out of the school gates, bouncing his soccer ball, Franklyn was lurking in the shadows. His glasses shone; his moist lips curved upward, spreading awkwardly across his face.

"Should we go down to the soccer field?" asked Luke.

"Not today, Luke. Don't you remember? Mother is expecting us!"

Luke inwardly cursed.

"Uh-oh. Sorry, but I can't come. I forgot to tell my mother, and she'll worry about where I am."

"That's no problem, Luke. She knows you always play soccer on Thursdays."

Luke was shuffling backward down the road.

"Um, it's just that I'd really like to, but I'm afraid . . ."

Franklyn was looking desperate.

"You've got to come. Mother's spent *days* baking. She'll be so upset."

Oh well, thought Luke grimly, might as well get it over with. After all, we do have exams next week, and if there are homemade goodies . . . He picked up the ball and shoved it in his backpack.

"Okay Franklyn, my man. Lead on."

"Oh, thanks, Luke. Thanks!"

They made an odd pair walking down the road: The tall blond boy in a sweatshirt and jeans, striding beside a miniature monk, this little, trotting, hooded person in a long black coat.

"Why do you always wear your hood, Franklyn?" teased Luke.

"I have a tendency to suffer from colds," said Franklyn with dignity. "Did you know that thirty percent of body heat is lost through the head?"

"I'll bet you wear a wool undershirt too."

"One should always wear natural fibers next to the skin; it's a scientifically proven fact that it's healthier."

"Hasn't done you much good, though, has it?"

"We are all made differently, Luke, and you shouldn't ridicule those different from yourself. Besides, the world isn't run by people like you, but by people like me."

Luke smiled down at the hood bobbing along beside him. "You may be right, pal. I'll settle for ruling the playground."

They had turned down a tree-lined avenue where the branches meshed overhead. It was chilly.

"Nearly there now," said Franklyn, glancing up at Luke. His face was green in the leaf-filtered light. The houses they were passing had an air of seedy respectability, of standards slipping but hanging on by their fingertips.

"Here we are." Franklyn pushed open a gate. There was a stone path leading to a small house. The bay window

6

was so overhung by the gable that though it was only half past four, there was a light behind the lace curtain. Luke thought he saw the curtain twitch, and then another light colored the stained-glass sunset in the front door. As they reached the step, the door popped open. For a second Luke felt like Hansel at the witch's cottage.

"You must be Luke!" said Mrs. Stone. "Come in, dear. It's such a pleasure to meet you."

She was nearly as small as her son, with a wide smile of perfect false teeth, echoing the row of false pearls around her neck. She wore a sensible skirt with an excessively sensible beige cardigan, buttoned to the neck; also a pair of offensively sensible shoes. Even grandmothers don't have to look like that nowadays, thought Luke.

"Step into the living room, boys, while I get the snacks. Everything is prepared."

Luke put his backpack on the hall stand and followed Franklyn. The living room was as trim as a dollhouse. By the window was a round table dressed in a frilly table-cloth. There were dishes and cake stands all over it, with cookies, jam sponge cakes, fruit cake, and little triangular sandwiches.

"You expecting an army?" said Luke.

Franklyn wiggled his fuzzy eyebrows anxiously as his mother brought in a tray.

"Well, isn't this nice?" She settled herself and started pouring tea. "Do you take sugar, Luke? There, I don't even know if you take sugar! So many things to learn about you! Now, you must tell me everything. It isn't often Franklyn brings home a little friend."

8

"Have some cake," urged Franklyn, seeing the panic in Luke's eyes.

Luke stolidly munched his way through everything in front of him, hoping that silence caused by a full mouth counted as good manners.

"What's your favorite subject?"

"What are your hobbies?"

"What are you going to do when you grow up?"

A team of interrogators skilled in the use of electrodes would have produced less misery.

"Well, I'm so glad you enjoy my cooking, dear. I do pride myself on my baked goodies, I must admit. Now, why don't you run along and play? Franklyn will show you his bedroom."

"Sorry about that," whispered Franklyn as they went into a back room. "I know she talks a lot. Here, sit down."

The room was dim, despite the wallpaper of large and aggressive roses. Fingers of ivy crawled down the window, strangling the light. Luke perched uneasily on the end of the bed as Franklyn switched on the bedside lamp. There were no posters, bunk beds with rumpled covers, broken toys, or muddy soccer shoes. This room had a single neat bed with a thin cotton bedspread, a table in the middle, and workbenches and shelves stacked with books and scientific equipment.

"What do you do with yourself on weekends?" asked Luke.

"As you can see, I have many interests. I've always got several experiments in progress." He gestured toward the table, where there was a tangle of tubes and bubbling vats. Luke averted his eyes from a jar of green liquid with something pulsating in it.

"I bet you'd be a whiz at computers," said Luke. "Or how about radio-controlled cars? They're real fun. You get the kit of Clodbuster, say, or Midnight Pumpkin, and make it yourself." Luke was warming to his favorite subject. "Tell you what, I've got a Thunderbird III that's great. If you help me with the exams, you can have that if you like; just for a start."

"Gosh, thanks, Luke. I was considering branching out into engineering and electronics when I finished biology."

"Don't you ever go out and have a good time? Swimming, movies, that sort of thing?"

"Mother doesn't like me to go to places where I might encounter germs, as my health is rather delicate. She only sends me to school because it's the law."

"But you haven't even got a TV!"

"Television saps the brain, Luke. Here, have a look at my botanical corner. Have you ever seen a Venus's-flytrap?" Franklyn pulled a potted plant from the small jungle in the corner.

"Yuck—it's got teeth," said Luke.

"That's right. You feed it flies." He reached for a jam jar, which was buzzing quietly. "Want to try?"

"No *thank* you, definitely not."

Luke moved up the bed, then jumped as his hand plunged into something furry.

"What's the matter, Luke? That's just my bedtime friend, Rutherford. I keep my pajamas on him."

"You're not such a nerd after all," Luke said, laughing

as he surveyed the collection of stuffed toys on the pillow. He picked up Rutherford, who was shaped like an orange cat with a zipper down the front.

"I've got a Garfield who's a little like this," he said. "Sometimes we pull him through the cat flap on a piece of string to scare our cat; he nearly has a heart attack. It's a real laugh." His voice trailed away as he looked closer at the cat's face.

"They are professional taxidermist's glass eyes," said Franklyn. "You can order them. Whenever my pets die, I like to preserve them if the pelt is in good condition. I've got a book on how to do it, if you're interested."

Luke hurriedly dropped Rutherford. He looked at the other bedtime friends—the cuddly puppy, that appealing floppy-eared bunny, and the guinea pig. . . .

"Come out to the back. I've got a big enclosure there, full of all sorts of animals you might like. Mother won't let them in the house when they're alive, because of the bacteria."

Luke looked at his watch as he edged toward the door.

"That's really nice of you, it's been really nice, but I've got to be getting on home now, it's definitely time. See you tomorrow, Franklyn."

He was stumbling down the hall, groping for his backpack.

"Are you leaving, dear?" Like a jack-in-the-box Mrs. Stone's head sprang around the living-room door.

"Thank you very much for having me, thank you for the snacks," he stammered. Jeez, he hadn't said that for years. A second later he was out the door and down the path. He was running through the darkening green tunnel of trees, away from that squat house with the blood-colored sunset in its door.

The next day Luke found it hard to meet Franklyn's eye; Franklyn really gave him the creeps. Never mind—exams were next week, then vacation, and next term he would be back beside Steven. He slid a lumpy shopping bag along the bench to Franklyn.

"Here it is," he said, "the Thunderbird like I promised. The remote control unit's a little out of shape, that's all."

Franklyn peered into the bag.

"Not exactly sophisticated, is it?" he said. "Those batteries, for instance. I'd give it a rechargeable electric unit, and miniaturize the control."

Luke put his hand out.

"If you don't like it, I'll take it back!"

"Oh, no, Luke, I'm grateful. You just wait and see what I do with it!"

Luke turned away and pretended to read his math book. He could see Steven's nose poking over his desk lid in their direction. Sure enough, at break Steven was waiting for him.

"What's that you gave old Franklyn?"

"Mind your own biz."

"He's your best friend now, isn't he?"

"What, that weirdo? Course not. No, you are."

"Why're you giving him stuff, then?"

Luke sighed. "Oh, all right. If you've gotta know." He explained about the exams, how his dad was going to give him a Clodbuster if he did well, and the only way to do well was to bribe Franklyn. Before he could stop himself, he was telling Steven about the gruesome afternoon he'd spent with Franklyn and his mother.

"That's really gross. That's disgusting. Hey, wait till I tell the others!"

Luke was seized with guilt.

"Don't do that, Steven, please. I shouldn't have snitched on him."

"It's your duty as a citizen. We can't have a murderer in the class, and no one knowing."

"Who says he murdered them?"

"Who says he didn't? It's like those doctors who did experiments for Hitler. Hey, Phillip, c'mere a minute. Guess what!"

Luke could have kicked himself. Bigmouth. Oh, well, too late now. During the next lesson he was aware of whispers, of notes passing. The rumor was cancerously spreading through the class, mutating and multiplying as it went.

On Monday morning he met Franklyn in the hall. "All set for the math test?" he asked.

For the first time they walked down the hall together. No one made any funny remarks, no one pointed. It's going to be all right, thought Luke. Probably they didn't believe Steven, or they weren't interested.

"Come down to the field later if you like," said Franklyn, "and see what I've made out of Thunderbird. I think you'll be impressed."

As they reached the classroom door, a bunch of boys pushed in ahead of them. For once the class was quiet.

Another peculiar thing, thought Luke, the kids were all on time. And the kids were all staring at him and Frank-lyn. All sitting at their desks, forty innocent faces spar-kling with anticipation. Luke and Franklyn walked to their desk, squarely in the middle of the front row. As they slid in, Luke saw. On the blackboard were the words:

FRanklyn Stone
Frankenstine
Stuff your pussycat
Dont stuff mine

There was a crude drawing of a cat with stitches in its forehead and a bolt through its neck. Oh, God. He turned his head. Franklyn's face was white, his teeth clenched. His eyes, black as beetles, glittered ferociously behind his glasses.

"You told them, didn't you?"

"I didn't mean to, Franklyn. Steve made me." It sounded pathetic.

"I thought I could trust you, but you're just like the others. You betrayed me, Luke. I won't forget it. I'll make you sorry for this—you'll see."

Through the gust of laughter, the snickering, braying uproar, Luke heard heels clipping down the hall. He scrambled out of the desk and grabbed the blackboard eraser. As Mrs. Milne came through the door, he was frantically smearing the chalk away, rubbing it to a white blur.

"Be QUIET, everybody. And what do you think you are doing, Luke? You know very well that you're not allowed to draw on the board. I expect you to stay behind this afternoon for detention. Now, pass around the papers for the math test."

As Luke slunk into his place, he tried to catch Franklyn's eye, but there was no response. He looked miserably at the questions in front of him. He couldn't answer any of them, and he didn't care.

There was another half hour of detention to go. Luke chewed his pen and watched a fly doing acrobatics. It landed on the window, and he gazed past it to the school landscape of worn grass and concrete, punctuated with potato-chip bags. It was hot, although the sky was gray. In fact, the sky was darkening by the minute, sagging to the concrete, merging with it. Beyond the buzzing of the fly, Luke thought he heard thunder. He looked hopefully at Mrs. Milne.

"All right, Luke. Just this once I'll let you off. It looks as if it's going to pour. I can give you a lift home at six, but I don't suppose you'll want to wait that long, will you?"

"Oh, no, Mrs. Milne. But thanks. I'll run all the way."

He crashed through the door into the hall. As he thudded toward the locker room, he noticed how unnaturally loud everything sounded in the deserted building. He couldn't find the light switch inside the door, so he felt his way through the lockers to the pegs. He could just make out their jagged, twiggy outlines against the frosted glass. There, at the end, were his things. He was eager to get out again; the place stank. He zipped up his jacket and was just pulling on the straps of his backpack when he heard something skittering behind him under the sinks. *Jeez*, rats, he thought, turning. He couldn't see anything at first; then two red spots glittered behind the shoe rack. He started to run toward the door, banging his knee as he looked back. There was a sheet of light for an instant, like a flash photo. As the thunder rumbled around his ears, Luke tried to make sense of what he had seen in that instant. Yes, there was something nasty under the sink; but there was also a shape hunched behind the door of the first toilet.

"Who's there?" he called as the thunder died away. Rain was falling now, drumming on the roof. Someone breathed out. Then that someone gave a high-pitched giggle.

"Just me, Luke, only me. Playing with Robo-Hamster. Want to meet him?"

"Come on, Franklyn, you gave me a real scare. What do you think you're up to? It's late."

"Don't patronize me, Luke. Show some respect for the creator of the world's first radio-controlled hamster."

"You're an ass, Franklyn. Look, I'm sorry about this morning. What more can I say? Forget it."

"Don't you call me an ass. I've got more brains in my little hamster than you've got in your entire body!"

Franklyn giggled again, a hysterical titter.

"Watch out, Luke. Beware the patter of tiny feet!"

16

Luke saw that the twin pinpricks of light were gliding across the floor toward him. Instinctively he rolled across the shoe rack and grabbed the handle of the playground door. It rattled uselessly in his hand; then he saw it was bolted at the top. As he reached up, tugging at the bolt, he felt a sharp pain in his ankle; there was something biting deep into his flesh, hanging on like grim death. He slammed his shoe hard against a locker, and whatever it was dropped squelchily onto the tiles. He opened the door and tore across the yard toward the gates. His left foot slopped warmly in its shoe as he ran, and spurts of pain flared up his leg. He saw a light in the classroom where Mrs. Milne was correcting exam papers and doubled back toward it. He could actually see her face, see her fingers holding an illicit cigarette, but there was no way he could get to her—the beast and its hooded master were out of the locker room and standing between them. He shouted, but the rain and thunder were louder still. There was nothing to do but to head for home. The pain made running hard, and he regretted all the training he'd given Franklyn, who was jogging comfortably along fifty feet behind him. Franklyn was insane, a psychopath—he must always have known it; it had been stupid, not kind, to tangle with this character.

He saw something moving from the corner of his eye, overtaking him, cutting him off. He swiveled sharply. There was Franklyn, smiling inside his hood. It was dark inside that hood. The shadow spread so far down that only the shapeless, mushy mouth could be seen—rosy in the streetlight, it was squirming gleefully.

"You can't go home, Luke. Hamster won't let you. He's better than a sheepdog. Better than a pit bull, actually."

He was holding the control unit.

"You'll catch cold, Franklyn. What will your mother say?"

"It'll be worth it, believe me. Come on, traitor, keep moving. Fast forward."

The rodent shot off again, skimming the slippery pavement. The sparse orange fur clung to its body in the rain, and Luke could see the sinews and muscles all working, as if it was still alive. It was circling him, making vicious little attacks to prod him in the right direction. It's crazy. I can't believe this, thought Luke. I'm being harassed by a hamster.

The streets were deserted—no one but a maniac (and his victim) would be out in such weather. Luke's vision narrowed to the path before him, which pointed into a black bowl of wind and rain. It felt as if he was running in place, as one identical streetlight after another swept past him; but he could not stop, in case the ribbon of path rolled him back to his tormentors. He stumbled on through unrelenting avenues of pain.

"We're going home, Luke," called Franklyn amiably, soothingly. "Nearly there; your troubles will soon be over."

Exhausted, Luke tripped and fell slithering across the sidewalk. As he raised his face, he saw, through the silver-needled night, a welcoming stained-glass sunset. Then he felt the creature scrambling up over his jeans, over his jacket. He caught a glimpse of curved yellow teeth before it reached his throat.

It was the last day of the term, and Mrs. Milne was organizing the clean-up. Funny, she thought, watching Luke make a neat pile of his books, what a good influence one child can have on another. It was one of her better ideas, putting those two together. Luke had done really well on his exams, apart from math, and his behavior had improved markedly. In this last week she'd noticed it particularly. Nowadays, he went everywhere with Franklyn; she'd even seen them going home together each afternoon. Franklyn, who had been such a sad, solitary little fellow, was definitely coming out of his shell, and was so much better for Luke than that dreadful Steven.

"Well, Franklyn!" she said, passing him a broom. "I see you've made yourself a new friend."

"That's right, Mrs. Milne. My most ambitious project so far."

Odd child! "Looking forward to next term, you two?" she joked.

"Yes, thank you, Mrs. Milne," they replied in unison.

Franklyn's mouth sprawled, and his little centipede eyes blinked up at her. Luke smiled too. The chiseled lips rearranged themselves in his handsome face as his eyes met hers; wonderful, bright-blue eyes, clear as glass.

Whenever the Wind Is High

Shelley and her brother were sitting outside of Dan's Bar and Grill when the Capri drove up. It was a magnificent machine; slick silver, with black stripes and chrome wire wheels. There was a green strip across the top of the windshield that read RAY over the driver's seat and CHERYL over the passenger's, and there was a window sticker, *If you drink, don't drive—you'll spill it.*

The children were eating burgers and french fries. As the car reversed into a parking space, Shelley tossed a fry that sailed over the vinyl roof and slid down the rear window to lodge on the spoiler.

"Hey! You kids got nothin' better to do?" yelled the driver, getting out and slamming the door. He hurled the fry back at her, took out a handkerchief, and polished furiously at the invisible grease mark.

"That sure is some cool dude," said Shelley sarcastically.

"Dressed to kill," agreed Mike.

The driver wore a gold chain around his neck, and gold rings. His jeans were as tight as sausage skins, his slicked-back hair as shiny as patent leather. He glared at them, then turned and strutted toward the bar.

"Does Cheryl know you're out?" Shelley shouted after him.

"Go home, you little brats," he called without looking back. "It's time for your mommy to tuck you in."

Mike wadded up the burger wrapper and sucked his fingers, one by one.

"It *is* getting late, Shelley. Do you think we should go now?"

"It's not that late. I think it's dark because it's starting to rain."

"If it rains, we'll have to go home anyway."

Shelley looked at her dinner; dark spots, flowering and merging, dotted the wrapper.

"There's no way I'm eating wet fries," she said. "Medallion Man forgot to lock up. Let's get in."

"In his precious car? You must be crazy! He'd flatten us."

"What he doesn't know. . . . Come on."

The tall seats were luxuriously covered with imitation tiger skin. Mike slid across to the passenger seat, and Shelley sat behind the wheel eating her burger. The rain was slanting down, bouncing off the hood, trickling around the windshield wipers. Mike reached out a finger to touch the dice that hung from the rearview mirror. They were large, pink, and furry, and it was soothing to watch them swinging, revolving gently. The windows were misting over as the car grew warmer, and Mike felt his eyes begin to close. Shelley poked him with her elbow.

"Don't poop out on me now, Mike. I want some fun."

21

She dropped her wrapper over the back of the seat and wiped her fingers on the tiger skin. "See what our flashy friend forgot, he was in such a hurry? The keys!"

Mike knew that his sister's tone of voice meant nothing but trouble. "I wanna go home," he whined.

"For Pete's sake, that's just like you. Remember when you were hooked on adventure game books, and I had to read them to you? Whenever we got to 'Do you want to fight the three-headed dragon, enter the ballroom of evil, or continue down the corridor?' you'd always choose the corridor. Whole books we'd go through, never getting out of that corridor. Well, this is our chance. I want a real adventure."

"But you can't drive!"

"Doesn't matter. It's automatic, see, just forward, backward, and stop. Even you could do it."

"Come off it, Shell. You can't even see over the wheel!"

"Give me your parka. No, fold it." She was impatient. "There, see? When I sit on it, no one outside can tell I'm not eighteen."

"I bet Cheryl doesn't have ketchup on her chin," Mike jeered.

"Shut up. I'm concentrating." She turned the key, and the engine—which was still warm—began to purr. Country and western music shrilled from speakers behind them as Shelley shifted gears and the car rolled forward. She felt around with her foot till she found a pedal and stepped on it. The car gave such a spectacular leap that she stamped on the other pedal; Mike's nose squashed into the windshield.

"Now you have a red chin too," said Shelley unsympathetically. "You'd better put on the seat belt. But wipe the windshield first. I can't see a thing."

He pulled off the furry dice and cleared swathes, like negative brushstrokes, across the misted glass. Visibility was hardly improved. Dan's Bar and Grill wavered and melted among the beads trickling down the windshield. Shelley pressed all the switches she could find until the wipers jerked into motion.

"Geronimo!" she cried. "Let's burn rubber!"

". . . so *very lucky, lucky lucky lucky,*" enthused a voice from the tape deck, as the Capri edged out of the parking lot leaving the merest hint of silver on the pole at the entrance. The car turned onto the divided highway toward town. As it gathered speed, Mike looked at Shelley, who was hunched forward, her tongue curling around her lip. He wiped his bloody nose on the back of his hand and noticed how white the knuckles were. What the hell, he thought. She's nearly thirteen. I suppose she knows what she's doing. He lay back against the tiger skin and consciously forced himself to relax. Might as well enjoy myself, he thought.

The speedometer said 70 mph, but the car zipped along as smoothly as a magic carpet. They were passing the industrial park—factories, wire fences, tire dumps, used-car lots, all dissolving in the gray rain. The streetlights came on, a trail of misty moons to the overpass. Mike suddenly found himself looking down on a line of traffic as the Capri crashed against the railings, rattling along for a few feet before bouncing back onto the road.

"Whoops!" said Shelley. "Just testing."

The road curved down again, and Mike saw the city center. Neon lights, like a scattered bag of candy, lay invitingly before them in the dusk.

"Shouldn't we slow down a little?" he asked diffidently.

"That's called backseat driving, and it's very bad manners," said Shelley. "Put on another tape; that's your job."

Mike fumbled with the player until the music changed. *Wyuld thying. Bom, ch ch, bom,* went the heavy beat. *Wyuld thying.* When he looked up, he saw that they had pulled up next to a Mack truck. A hand's breadth away was the angry face of a middle-aged man in a hat, his mouth opening and closing. He's trying to tell us something, thought Mike, but we can't hear because of the glass. I wonder if that's what my goldfish is doing.

"Are you sure this is still a divided highway?" he asked Shelley.

"Trust me!"

She accelerated to avoid a truck that loomed, head-on, in the mist. "One of those foreign drivers probably."

In the mirror Mike saw the truck stuck halfway up the bank beside the road. He twisted around to get a better view, but it was already out of sight. He tried to look in the store windows, but they were gone too quickly. Passersby, glimpsed in a slivered instant, were as frozen in action as the models in the windows; both turned pale, flat faces toward the Capri as it flashed past.

"Where are we going?" Mike asked.

"The expressway. The open road, see what this little baby can really do."

"It says one twenty on the dial."

"Wowee. That's twice what we're doing now!" She was bouncing up and down on the seat.

"You're supposed to stop for people," he reproached, as a group in evening dress scattered across the road.

"It wouldn't be safe to stop at this speed, especially with all those puddles," Shelley said.

"The puddles have disappeared now—they're on the people," said Mike.

In fact, the rain was beginning to clear. A stiff breeze tore at the antenna and scraped the clouds from the sky. As they reached the summit of the next hill, they saw a fanfare of stars shimmer across the woods and hills.

"Whoa, over we go!" shouted Shelley, and put her foot down. The car veered into the fast lane, gobbling up the white lines faster and faster. Mike could see nothing but that white thread winding up, everything else a blue-black smear of speed. He felt sick.

"You all right?" asked Shelley. He opened his eyes and looked out the window.

"Are we in another country now?" he asked.

"Course we're not, silly."

"Then why have the signs got such strange names? I've never heard of a place with a name like 'Lville' or 'Bmham.' You can't even say them."

"Maybe we're in Canada. Shh a minute. Turn the music down." Shelley had heard the sirens before he had. She swore.

"Where are they, Mike? I'll try and lose them."

Mike looked back and saw three or four flashing red lights on the brow of the last hill.

"You'll have to get a move on," he said. "For one thing, we're nearly out of gas."

"We'll take the first turn-off," said Shelley.

Final Exit, the sign read. A32 to Hll.

"Hell?" suggested Mike.

"Hull, probably," said Shelley.

It was a smaller, ill-lit road. The surface was rough, and the car shuddered. Mike could feel the wind buffeting the windows as the car rose to higher ground. He looked back down the shiny road to where it dived into blue cauliflower treetops; there was neither sight nor sound of the police cars.

"Those fancy new sirens—they're just pretending to be cops," sneered Shelley, but she didn't slacken speed. It was exhilarating up on the top of the world, beating through the wind on moon-bleached hills as bare as bones, stretching in all directions. The highway lights were gone, and the only human mark was a clump of pylons and telephone poles, blackly crisscrossed with power lines, on a far hill. Mike, for some reason, felt better.

"What's that noise?" said Shelley suddenly, startling him. There was a faint rumble, like an underground railway.

"It can't be a train," said Mike. "The rhythm's all wrong."

"Maybe the engine's dying," Shelley said. Mike pulled himself up again to peer down the road. He blinked and shook his head, and sat down with a thump.

"Well?" said Shelley, irritated.

"You are not going to believe this."

"Try me."

The rumble turned to thunder and Shelley sensed a powerful mass moving beside her window. She glanced to her left, and the car swerved.

"Did you see what I saw?" she squeaked, gripping hard on the wheel.

"Yup," said Mike.

"A horse!" She sounded more outraged than surprised. "Doing a hundred miles an hour!"

Mike looked over and up through her window at the legs where they joined the chest and haunches, moving as smoothly and regularly as pistons. The muscles glistened with sweat in the moonshine. He wondered if Shelley had noticed there was a man's leg too, its booted foot in a stirrup. As he watched, the boot rose with a flash of metal, and squeezed the brown flank. There was a ripple of muscle as the horse accelerated, the body rising and falling until it drew ahead of the car. The strong hind-quarters were in front of them, the tail flowing back toward the windshield. And from above the horse, from a shadowy form, billowed waves of undulating blackness.

"What the hell is THAT?" asked Shelley.

"A cloak," said Mike. "I hate to say it, but I think he's a highwayman."

Shelley, for the first time, put on the brakes. The horse and rider wheeled to face them as the Capri slowed and stopped. Man and horse stood as one beast, the cloak whipping around them. Apart from a sharp crescent of cheekbone under the three-cornered hat, the children could see no face.

Mike got out. The ground felt unsteady beneath his feet, as if he'd been at sea too long, and the wind knocked him sideways. He put a hand on the door to steady himself and saw Shelley getting out the other side. Farther down the road the highwayman swung a leg over the horse and jumped down. He poked a bony finger toward them and swiveled it upward, beckoning.

"What do you want?" called Shelley, walking around the car to hold Mike's hand. "Who are you?"

"I am Black Jack, young mistress." His voice was wheedling, reedy as the wind. "There is a place I want to show you. Come, follow me."

"Not a chance," said Shelley. "Mike, we're going home now."

"We can't; there's not enough gas. I'm scared, Shelley."

"Let's get in the car and lock the doors." She reached for the door handle, but the wind snatched it from her grasp, slamming the door. The highwayman was loping down the road toward them. It was hard to tell how close he was, the black outline changing drastically as the cloak swelled and shrank like the tide. Wind-blown tears blurred Mike's eyes, and his nose started to run. He sniffed. Shelley squeezed his hand and spoke, but the wind stole her words.

The man stood tall before them. He stretched down and took their hands in his; small, warm pads crushed in fingers like iron. He led them along the road. There was no point in resisting. They ran to save the drag on their arms, and to keep pace with his long strides. As they passed the horse—head down, reins swinging—Mike saw they had reached the hill of telephone poles.

The highwayman pulled them off the pavement onto the soft, short grass dotted with sheep droppings.

"What do you see?" he demanded. They were looking into a forest of poles. The wires were humming, and there was a quiet bump-bumping as the wind swung the dark things that hung from the poles, nudging them against the wood.

"Shall I tell you what you see?" he hissed gleefully. "A Rogues' Gallery!" The children, coming closer, saw that on every pole a corpse dangled, a rope around its neck. Some of them, recently dead, hung heavily; their shoes were shiny, and there were still creases in their pants. Others were as light and dry as driftwood, where bone shone white through skin and matted hair. With each gust of wind they swayed together, rags fluttering, shoes clattering against the tarred poles.

The highwayman dragged the children between the hanging bodies and up the hill. Shelley and Mike slithered on the wet grass, but he did not slow, his fingers tight around their wrists now. Mike looked down, trying not to see pair after pair of dangling feet, until they reached the bare summit. An explosion of crows flapped coarsely away.

"Death lies at the end of the road for every man," intoned the highwayman. "Why would you speed upon your way and arrive untimely at that destination?"

Mike was crying.

"I don't understand you," said Shelley, "or what this place is, or what you want with us."

The highwayman extended a finger to point down the hill. Poles sprang, thick as porcupine quills, down the round hillside to the highway shoulder. They could see the horse grazing there, where the grass was clear. Beyond him, cars in endless procession slid past in the hazy lights.

"See how fast they go, the rascals of the road?" said the highway man. "Too fast to see the gallows, too fast to heed my dolls of fortune who hang in horrid warning."

As they watched, a truck lurched sideways, a tire blown. Behind it a sleek dark car, the car of a businessman, glided into a skid. Others joined the dance, spinning, waltzing gracefully along the highway till they all embraced in a glory of flame.

"Soon they will be with us on the hill," gloated the highwayman, cracking his knuckles. "Another fine brace of villains for my hunting bag."

"But it was all just an accident!" Shelley protested, shocked.

"An accident, my lady?" shrieked the highwayman. "An accident? The first villain had overladen his cart, and had not gotten sleep; the second villain drove his carriage too fast, and too close, and as for the third villain—why, he had drunk too much ale. And you call that an accident, mistress? Let their bodies swing, I say, what is left of them. They are better here, where they can claim no blameless lives."

Mike's lip wobbled. "Do you mean to say Shelley and me are dead too?"

The highwayman looked down at him. He raked his fingers delicately through the boy's hair.

"I may yet spare you; lads and lasses are not my favorite meat. If you have learned your lesson well, the wind may blow you home to bed."

As the nightmare faded, Shelley was crying out, "But please, what about the car, it isn't ours, can you . . . ?"

The last thing she saw was teeth grinning beneath the nodding three-cornered hat.

It was closing time at Dan's Bar and Grill. Ray Ramsden, proud Capri owner, swaggered out into the night and belched contentedly. He was a bit unsteady on his feet, but wasn't worried. Once behind the wheel, he told himself, there's nothing like a few beers to boost the old driving skills, to add a bit of dash and verve. He felt his pockets for the keys. Damn, had he lost them? He stumbled a few steps back toward the bar, then a thought struck him and he tried the car door. It was unlocked, and, of all horrors, he'd left the keys in the ignition. Lucky it was still here—but then he'd always been a lucky guy. He got in and sniffed; he could smell french fries. Somebody had been inside! He checked the glove compartment and found nothing missing. The German shepherd with the nodding head was still on the rear window, and the Spanish Lady, under the stick-on Garfield. Still, there was something different about the car. His dice! His lucky pink dice had been swiped. Who on earth would do such a thing? He squinted into the gloom and thought he saw something hanging where the dice had been. He opened the door, so that the light went on, and saw—or was it a trick of the light?—an old-fashioned wax doll, tied by a string around its neck to the rearview mirror. It had black silk hair and a gold chain. A breeze swirled around the parking lot and the doll began to swing, its feet tapping as they turned.

Secrets

Or, The Curse of Estragon

It's been five years since it happened, but I still remember it as clear as yesterday. We'd been in the new housing development for only a couple of weeks; and when I say new, I mean new. Woodland Crescent, where we lived, was a mud plain with occasional lines of brick laid out for the new homes, looking like ancient remains. Our house was the first to be finished, and the yard was still marked out with posts and string when we moved in.

The inside of the house was fine, though. Mom and Dad were thrilled with the teak-style custom kitchen, and the magnolia walls and eggplant carpeting. (Before that, we'd been in the same kind of housing project we live in now.)

Anyway, one Saturday morning I was sitting at the breakfast table eating my cornflakes. My older brother, Steve, was beside me, eating sloppily because, as usual, he had a book in one hand.

"Will you play with me after breakfast?" I asked him. I was only seven at the time.

"Too busy."

"No you're not, you're only reading," I said. "We could play hide-and-seek."

"You need more than two people for hide-and-seek, and besides, the yard's a swamp."

Mom chipped in. "Steve, please get your nose out of a book for once and think about someone else."

Sucking on his spoon, he put the book down and looked at me thoughtfully.

"I won't play with you," he said slowly, "but I will tell you a very big secret. If you solemnly promise not to tell anyone."

"I won't snitch, honest."

He looked at me sideways.

"On second thought, you're too young. It wouldn't be fair to you."

"Cross my heart and hope to die," I pleaded. I was getting excited. He glanced across at Mom, who was playing with the garbage disposal.

"Come into the living room, then. It's more private."

He sat in the armchair, and I sat on a footstool, looking up at him eagerly.

"Shut the door," he ordered. "Okay. Are you ready for it?"

I nodded.

"Well then. The fact is, this development is actually the medieval estate of Estragon, and"—he leaned forward—"the entrance to a castle is under this very house. But I can't tell you any more than that."

"Get out of here!" I shouted. "You're fooling me."

"Shhhh! Keep your voice down. I knew I shouldn't have told you. Still, if you don't believe me, maybe it's just as well."

"A medieval castle? But it's all new houses around here, all modern."

"But what was here in the old days, dumbo? You know there's that ancient wall near the town center, and the burial mounds in the mall are even older."

He was convincing me.

"Why's it a secret, anyway?"

"Because of the curse. The builders know about it, but they're keeping quiet, or no one would buy the houses."

"You're kidding me—what curse?"

"There's a wizard in the castle called Mandrake. Mandrake the Malevolent. And he's cursed the fair princess, Esmerelda. She won't marry him, so he's imprisoned her for all eternity. And he's cursed the whole development."

"You're a nut case," I said doubtfully. "All right, then show me. Prove it."

"I'm not sure I want to now. I'm not sure you're a suitable person. You're what's called a skeptic."

He's clever—Steve knows just about everything.

"Also, you may not want to go there when I tell you something really scary. Are you sure you want to hear?"

I nodded wildly, my mouth open.

"Well then, Mandrake has the power to turn men to stone. If you look in his face, it's instant. The castle is littered with the frozen bodies of unwary adventurers."

This stunned me for a minute.

He went on. "Tell you what, though. I've got an idea.

35

You wear a blindfold, and I'll lead you."

"But what if *you* see Mandrake?" I asked nervously.

"Umm . . . I'll take Dad's shaving mirror and walk backward. Wait here."

I sat on the footstool, chewing my nails and banging my knees together. Outside the window, bulldozers carved the land, ruthlessly trundling over the battleground of history. I was overcome with the wonder of it all.

In a minute he was back. He closed the door secretively, looked over his shoulder, then emptied a shopping bag onto the carpet. There was a red and white striped scarf and hat, a mirror, and a carving knife. I got even more excited at the sight of the knife. I was jumping up and down.

"You're not going to kill anyone, are you, Steve?"

"I hope not. No, no, the dagger is just a precaution, in case we run into trouble."

I gasped.

"Come here." He was impatient. "Close your eyes."

I felt the scarf going around and around my head and being tied in a tight knot. The hat followed, pulled all the way down to my chin.

"I can't breathe!" I mumbled. He rolled it up as far as my mouth.

"Did you see that?" he checked.

"What?" It was blacker than night from where I was looking.

"Fine." He took my hand and led me into the front hall. "We have to turn six times," he whispered, "and chant the mystic word *Asphodel.*" His hands were on my shoulders, steadying me, but I felt as if my brain was spinning as the ancient magical forces took me in their power. My brother's hands made me still again.

"On your knees," he instructed, still whispering, "and crawl straight forward through the time tunnel."

I hesitated, and he shoved me in the back. I crawled, feeling the carpet under my hands change suddenly to boards. He turned me again and pulled me up.

"Do you want to climb the stairway to the turret or have a look at the dungeons?" He sounded like the real-estate agent who had sold us the house.

"I can't look at anything with this stuff on," I pointed out.

"Well, no, but I can describe it to you."

I heard clashing and clanging, a little like someone doing dishes.

"Is that the dungeon?" I asked.

"It sounds as if they're using the Iron Maiden today," he replied. "I think we'll skip that. Let us ascend to the battlements instead."

"It's getting really hot under this stuff," I complained, tugging at the scarf as he led me upward.

"Stop moaning, you big baby. It's freezing with these thick stone walls—you don't know how lucky you are. And it's me who's running all the risks, I'll thank you to remember."

We reached the top.

"There's a chamber on the left," he breathed in my ear, "where Mandrake dwells with his raven. And a toad. While to our right lies the maiden's turret. The choice is yours."

"Wouldn't it be safer to see Esmerelda?" I whispered.

37

I heard him push a door and move past me. After a second he drew me in after him.

"It's okay; she can't see us. She's sitting up in the gallery, looking out the window to see if any knight is galloping across the estate to save her. She's spinning flaxen thread. Oh, I wish you could see her stockings of carnation silk, her sumptuous damask gown laced with gold to complement her hair, her cheek, that fair garden wherein the lily vies with the rose . . . Watch the chest."

I rubbed my shins, trying not to cry out, and fumbled my way back through the door.

"Listen!" hissed Steve urgently. "I hear the croak of the raven." He grabbed my hand and pulled me briskly down the stairs. We crawled through the time tunnel, then revolved, chanting *Asphodel.* I tore off the blindfold and used it to wipe the sweat from my face. As I blinked, my eyes focused on the hall stand, with the phone, and the boots underneath.

"Do you believe me now?" demanded Steve. We were both panting. I nodded, unable to speak. He cupped his hand against my ear. "The entrance," he whispered, "is through the closet under the stairs. I'll tell you that much. But don't try it on your own. You know you wouldn't survive for a second."

"Will you take me again?" I begged.

"Tomorrow. If you go away now, play by yourself for a while, and let me finish my book."

I could only get him to take me on weekends; and between these, at school, I was finding it hard to concentrate. It seemed so silly making plastic models and reading about Meg the Hen when I was in touch with the actual cosmic forces of evil, unraveling the mystery of time itself. I told no one. At break I crouched in the corner by the hall steps, brooding, until my friends gave up on me. I felt a thousand years older than them. I could think about nothing but saving the princess.

My parents noticed the change in me.

"Moving's always disruptive for children," I heard Mom telling Dad. "A new neighborhood, and so forth. Not that you could call this mess a neighborhood."

"I'll get some charcoal for Saturday," said Dad. "Would that cheer you up, Danny? A barbeque and bonfire? There's a big fireworks display in town too."

"Good idea," applauded Mom. "A housewarming!"

So we didn't have time to go to the castle on the day it all happened, because Dad took us into town to get stuff for the barbeque, and then we had to collect wood for the bonfire. It was weird roaming the development in the foggy dusk. It was like a bombed city, with the jagged walls and the mud. The silence was creepy too. The pickings were rich, though, and as it grew dark we pushed a big haul home in an old wheelbarrow. Mom was stacking the wood.

"It's very damp," she said. "I hope we're not going to have trouble with the fire." She crumpled a lot of newspaper and stuffed it in the gaps in the wood, then broke up the packing crates and put them on top. "Praise be, we won't be needing these again!" she rejoiced, squirting on the lighter fluid.

Mom lit the newspaper. The bonfire took off with a whoosh, blazing to the sky, and we cheered. Then she brought out some baked potatoes, which we ate while Dad barbequed. We didn't get to bed till after ten because we played tapes when we got in and danced around. It was like a real party.

When we did get to bed, I was too excited to sleep, and I started thinking about the castle again. We'd been there about half a dozen times now, and it was obvious that Steve wasn't going to do anything about Esmerelda. It was clearly up to me—I would have to be the brave knight to gallop across the estate of Estragon.

Creeping out of the lower bunk so I wouldn't wake Steve, I put on my bathrobe and slippers. I went to the bathroom to get the shaving mirror, but when I tried to walk downstairs looking into it, I nearly fell over backward. Clinging to the bannisters, I heard the mirror bounce to the bottom and roll against the front door.

"What the hell's going on?" came a blurred, sleepy voice from upstairs.

"Just went to the bathroom," I called back. Well, it wasn't a lie. I decided I'd be safer with the scarf over my eyes, feeling my way. But first, the equipment had to be assembled. I put the knife in a shopping bag, plus newspapers, matches, and a new can of lighter fluid. Through the kitchen window I saw a rocket explode and fountain down, far away across the barren wastes of the development; it seemed a good omen for my quest.

The hall was so dark, I hardly needed the blindfold, but I put it on anyway. "*Asphodel*," I intoned, turning, then slung the bag over my shoulder and felt for the handle of the hall closet. I crawled in. I could feel the vacuum cleaner, some bottles, a dustpan and brush, and circled carefully, desperate not to knock anything over. Then I felt air on my face again and crawled through the opening. The turret staircase was, I knew, on the left. I groped my way up, sticking close against the wall to avoid the crumbling masonry. My plan was bold and simple.

At the top of the steps, I felt for the left-hand door where Mandrake dwelled, then stood, listening, for at least a minute. There was a faint, regular snuffling. So Mandrake was asleep. I pushed the door, which creaked open, but the breathing didn't falter. It seemed best not to use the newspaper because of the noise the crumpling would make. I felt my way around, counting my steps, till I came across a wall hanging. Aha, I thought, the great hunting tapestry; this should burn fast. I put the bag down softly and unscrewed the lighter fluid can. When the fabric was well soaked, I stepped back six paces, judging that I was halfway to the door.

I struck a match, knowing by the warmth on my fingers that it was lit, and tossed it at the tapestry. Just to be on the safe side, I struck a whole handful and threw them too. There was a crackling, and a red, warm glow spread through the scarf and over my eyelids.

Done it! I thought. Now I've just got to lock Mandrake in and wake the princess. I started tiptoeing out, but crashed into a piece of furniture and fell over. I completely lost my sense of direction. I didn't dare take the scarf off. I was sure the noise must have woken Mandrake, but I just kept crawling around on my hands and knees looking for the door. The heat was searing, and smoke thick as cotton was tumbling down my throat, stuffing my lungs. Nothing, not even turning to stone, could be worse

than suffocation. I pulled at the scarf, clawing my face free, and looked around the room.

But what had happened to the four-poster bed carved with griffons? Where were the pointed, latticed windows, and the shelf with the skulls? Above all, where was Mandrake the Malevolent, with his back humped under an ermine cape? I was looking at a bedroom with two bunk beds and a bureau.

The room was lit by blazing curtains, which sent waves of flame lapping over the curtain rod to the ceiling. The teddy bears on the windowsill were haloed with fire, and a rubber Smurf was melting, dripping hideously onto the carpet. That was on fire too, and the electric train tracks were writhing and buckling from the heat. Behind them, our new wallpaper was curling up from the wainscoting.

"Steve!" I called. "Please wake up!"

The blankets stirred on the top bunk, and I saw his face through the smoke, red lit, with black shadows over the cheeks.

"Fire!" I shrieked. "FIRE!"

Well, we all got out all right. In fact, I was quite a hero for raising the alarm. But what with the fireworks in town, and the development being unlit and unmarked, by the time the fire trucks arrived, the house was gutted. It wasn't insured, either. Maybe Steve was right about the curse. As to how the fire started, well, that's my secret.

Many Happy Returns!

The man had a nail through his head—it was a long one that went in one side and came out the other. Apart from this he was very ordinary, in a baggy gray suit lightly sprinkled with dandruff and cigarette ash.

"Come in, young man. You're letting in the flies," he said.

The boy held up a bright package. "I've brought this for Mark." He was on his best behavior, and that did not include screaming and running up the front path.

"You'd better go and find him, then, shouldn't you? And is your lovely mother coming in?" He smirked over the boy's head.

"I'll pop in for a minute, just to say hello," said Sally.

With a courtly bow and a flourish of the hand, the entertainer ushered them into the hall.

"Yoohoo, Jan," called Sally, squeezing past him.

"I'm in the kitchen," came the reply.

The doorbell rang, and the boy watched the magician go to answer it. He could see now that the nail was actually in two pieces, joined by a piece of plastic that curved around the head. He decided that the purpose of the nail was to secure a wide mat of hair that stretched from one ear to the other, and to divert attention from it. He wondered why anyone would make such a structure.

"Don't stare. It's rude," whispered Sally, and went on with her conversation.

"Mr. Smarty-Pants? I don't think I've heard of him. Who was he recommended by?"

"Well, no one, I'm afraid," Jan said. "The agency says it's always murder in June; we were lucky to get anyone at all. I hope he'll be okay."

"Of course he will. Of *course* he will. Cheer up, it's only once a year. All right then, I better get going."

"Oh," said Jan. "Wouldn't you like to stay for a while?"

"What's the matter?"

"Well . . . Mark wanted the whole class, that's thirty kids. I don't even know half of them! And that old fellow doesn't really look up to it."

"And you could use some moral support? Say no more. I'll help you take those desserts in."

By the time they had set the table, the house was overflowing with children.

"There can't possibly be any more, can there?" said Sally.

"I hope not. There's the bell again. I'll get it."

On the step, all alone, stood a little boy. He was thoughtfully picking his nose.

"Where's your mom?" asked Jan.

"I always come by myself. I'm Neville."

"You'd better come in, then," said Jan, noticing that he hadn't brought a present, and that his nails were the dirtiest she'd ever seen. "The others are all in the dining room waiting for the magic to begin. This way."

The children were sitting on the floor by the open French windows. Against one wall the entertainer was laying out cloths and boxes, the tricks of his trade, and against the other wall was a table of potato chips and dip and candies and cake . . .

"Mom!" called Mark. "That strange boy, he's—"

"Candles!" she cried. "Wait a minute." When she'd gotten them, she couldn't resist lingering in the doorway to enjoy the scene. She felt utter satisfaction. It was the sort of moment, she thought, one remembers when they are grown: the children all dressed so prettily, their little faces bright with excitement and expectation, their chatter mingling with the summer sounds of bees and a distant lawn mower . . . and was that the tinkle of a fountain? She looked over their heads and to the backyard.

"Neville!" she screeched. "Stop that at once! NOT in the sandbox, if you please!"

The entertainer cleared his throat.

"Are we sitting comfortably?" he said, wearily raising his hands to quiet them. "Then I shall begin. Who'd like to choose a card?" His voice swelled to drown the yelps of those with fingers crushed by Neville on his ruthless way to the front.

"It's a three of hearts," said Neville.

"You peeked!" said another child.

"No I didn't. Bet you anything the whole pack is threes of hearts."

"Shhh!" said Jan. The entertainer went on grimly with the trick.

"Boys and girls, you will never guess what this card is."

"The three of hearts," they shouted in unison, and giggled.

"Quiet, please, let's have a little quiet," implored Jan. The entertainer started taking colored scarves from a box.

"I am about to perform a most peculiated and compuliar trick," he said, wafting them through the air. "Can you guess what I will do with these pretty things?"

The children all looked at Neville.

"What, no toilet paper?" enquired Neville politely.

"I shall eat them," said Mr. Smarty-Pants, addressing a little girl at the farthest point from Neville. He crumpled them up and put them into his mouth. When he pulled them out again, lo and behold, they were all tied end to end in a rope. There was an impressed gasp; then they turned to look at Neville.

"He's got them up his sleeve. Look, up his left arm."

Next came the disappearing-rabbit trick. The children, who had been getting raucous, calmed down a little. They liked the rabbit.

"It doesn't really disappear, you know," chipped in Neville. "It's in a compartment at the back of the box."

"Did you ever wonder," said the entertainer, slowly and clearly, "why you were given a name with the word 'vile' in it?"

"What *we* was wondering," replied Neville, "is how you got the name Smarty-Pants when you're not in the least bit smart."

He began to chant, "Smarty-Pants, Smarty-Pants, Smarty-

47

Pants . . ." only instead of the word "Smarty," he used a word that rhymed with it. The children howled with laughter and joined in.

"That's enough!" cried Jan. "Neville, please go and wait in the kitchen until cake time. I don't like to get cross at parties, but when poor Mr. Far—I mean, Smarty-Pants has been kind enough to come and entertain us . . ."

"Dear lady, do not concern yourself. My fee is your freedom. Just sit back and enjoy the show."

He stretched out his arms dramatically.

"Do you all know what an illusion is? Now you see it, now you don't? Good. Girls and boys, ladies, I shall now perform the greatest illusion the world has ever seen. Would the troublesome young gentleman care to assist?"

Neville stood up and sauntered toward the magician. A hush fell. The boy grinned over his shoulder, then said challengingly, "Yeah? Go on, then."

"First I need three chairs," said Mr. Smarty-Pants.

Jan and Sally passed them to him. He arranged them so that two were facing each other and one was sideways in the middle.

"Lie down, young man."

Neville lay along the chairs, his feet sticking between the slats. He turned his face to the audience, crossed his eyes, and stuck out his tongue.

"I think we could do without the sight of your charming features," said the magician. He placed a pole across the tops of the chairs on the audience side, and flung a cloth over it so that it hung down to form a curtain. It was a fine cloth made of purple velvet with gold tassels all around—an odd contrast to the dirty shoes sticking out.

"Now!" he said, reaching into his bag. "What have we here?"

The children sat up eagerly.

"We have a rare and precious sword, a golden sword, which was used over many centuries by the kings of Persia for executions. Can you all see?"

He held it at arm's length, moving it slowly from side to side. It glittered fiercely in the sunlight.

"And it's very sharp. You see this hot dog?" He leaned over and took one from the table. "Hold this, little girl. No, stick your arm out. That's it."

He swung the sword in a great arc that ripped the air with a hiss; half a hot dog toppled, like a severed finger, onto the child's satin party dress. She began to sob, and Jan pulled her up on her knee for a hug.

"Oh, dear," she whispered to Sally, "do you think this is safe?"

"Of course it is. He's a professional, isn't he? They have to belong to a magic union, or something."

"Hush, ladies," he reproached them. "Now, to continue; when I give the signal, I want you all to say the magic words:

>   The sky is blue, but blood is red.
>   Magic sword chop off his head!

"Have you all got that?"

"Yes!" they shouted exultantly.

"All right then. All together now."

The windows rattled as thirty children bellowed the rhyme. Slowly, majestically, the entertainer lifted the

49

sword higher and higher. He seemed to swell, to grow in stature, filling the room with his presence, like a priest in some demonic rite. The sword was nearly touching the ceiling . . . then it flashed down. There was a slight *snick*. The muddy shoes twitched violently and fell slack. From under the cloth a slim white forearm slipped toward the floor until the hand rested on the carpet, the fingers curving gracefully upward. A dark liquid trickled down the chair leg, the stain spreading evenly across the carpet.

The audience gasped. The mothers, after a moment, turned to each other. Jan pushed her fist against her mouth. She was shaking.

"Calm down, don't panic," whispered Sally. "We have to get the children into the yard. You get them out, and I'll pull the curtains."

"Oh, Christ!"

"Pull yourself together. Come on, quickly; they might not realize."

A child screamed. "Look, look, it's blood!" Another screamed, and another.

Sally was shouting, "Just a little scratch, nothing to worry about. Come along now, we'll play some nice games in the backyard."

She was pushing them frantically through the doors. At first they didn't move, stupid as sheep, then they stampeded. She turned her back to pull the curtains. The magician was slumped in an armchair. He was patting his pockets and frowning. He stuck his hand in a jacket pocket and pulled out a mouse, which he looked at vaguely, then put on the carpet. Poking around in the pocket again, he produced a cigarette, which he lit, lying back in the chair.

The mouse scuttled across the room and climbed up onto the table; it picked up a potato chip and began to nibble delicately. It had left red footprints on the white tablecloth.

Sally swallowed hard. She dragged the curtains across the windows and stepped out, closing the doors. The children were all waiting, pressed up against the fence at the end of the backyard. Jan gripped her arm.

"What'll I tell his mother?" she kept saying.

"You're hurting me," said Sally. "For God's sake, stop being so hysterical. The mothers will be here in a minute. You've got to look after the children while I phone for an ambulance. Not that there's much point. Oh, and I'd better call the police too, I suppose."

"But how will I tell the poor little boy's mother? It's too awful—I just can't do it."

"Don't worry, the police'll see to that. Now, get a hold of yourself. I'm going back in there."

It took all her courage to force herself to go through the doors. She pulled the curtains apart and stepped inside.

As her eyes grew used to the darkened room, Sally saw that the entertainer was packing away his things. The chairs on which the boy had lain were lined up against the wall.

"What have you done with him?" she demanded. "Where's the boy? I warn you, I'm going to call the police."

"He always comes," said the magician. "Nasty little so-and-so. Makes my life a misery."

"But you *killed* him. He was just a child!"

"Oh, that was years ago. About twenty, I'd say. And it

really was an accident, I promise you. But the little brat won't let me alone. Perhaps he's waiting for me to improve, so he can't guess the tricks. Ha!" He stubbed out the cigarette in some dip, which fizzed.

"Are you telling me . . . are you saying that he's a ghost?" she asked hesitantly.

"That's right. Well, sweetie, you couldn't get stains like that off a carpet, could you?"

She looked at the carpet, at the tablecloth; they were spotless.

"There is one thing I'll say, though," he said, smiling roguishly and adjusting the nail. "You must admit it was a wonderful illusion!"

Decorating the Bridge

Y ou mean to tell me you haven't got a 0-6-0 pan-
nier tank No. 7700? It's a standard, son, it's ba-
sic." The familiar voice fluted from the other end
of the store.

"A 7701? A 7701! My dear boy, do you know nothing?
For a 0-1 gauge railway it's got to be your 7700, or it's no
use, no use whatsoever."

Josh caught my eye, and the corners of his mouth
drooped.

"Isn't that Mr. Ramsbottom?" said my mother. "I'll just
go over and say hello."

We trailed furtively behind her. Mr. Ramsbottom
glanced at Mom and continued, "A 0-6-1 is perfectly useless for my purpose, do you understand, young man? Do I
make myself clea—" He did a double take, then turned
into a quivering heap of body language.

"It's Mrs. . . . er . . . Rignall, isn't it?" His fingers
twined anxiously in those odd tufts of hair on top of his
head. Parents always have this effect on him, especially
the richer ones, the mothers with red high-heeled shoes

and smiles flashy as a BMW bumper.

"I just wanted to thank you," said Mom, "for helping Bryan with his work. We were delighted with his results in religion."

"Oh . . . oh . . . well, imparting knowledge to the young, you know, is a very special privilege."

It's true, I got a seventy in religion this term. It's the only subject I got more than a twenty for. What Mom doesn't know is that I was down at the freight yards that day. She doesn't know Ramsbottom has given up any hope of imparting knowledge to the young, and gives us all good marks in the hope of keeping his job. She is unaware that he comes back from lunch break a little bit wobbly but considerably happier and unable to pronounce "Ezekiel." You know Mallet's Mallet, that word association game? Well, we've got a version where the person to get to "Ramsbottom" first wins. For instance, say you started with "window," it might go: "Window, glass, whisky, RAMSBOTTOM!" Or: "Window, pane, spanking, RAMSBOTTOM!" Any vice or depravity will do.

Actually, I believe his name's really Mr. Woolias, Richard Woolias, but for obvious reasons it's changed to Ramsbottom, and over the years he's given up trying to change it back.

"So you collect model trains?" asked Mom politely.

"My secret passion," twinkled Ramsbottom.

So that's it! He was warming to her, sweating into his mustache. "I have a superb 55XX class 2-6-2T locomotive, which is electrically operated through a stud contact system. It gives me hours of pleasure."

"How fascinating!"

55

"Really? Are you interested in model trains? Maybe you'd like to come up to my apartment and see my layout?"

"Well, thank you, Mr. Ramsbottom, that would be lovely. I'm always trying to get Bryan to take up a hobby; maybe that will inspire him."

We left without buying a computer game, which is what we were there for, and trekked down Main Street behind Mom and Ramsbottom. He lived nearby, in a big old house on a side street. As we climbed the stairs, we heard arguing and banging doors, while the smells ranged from boiled cabbage to curry. Not exactly a great apartment block, more a pile of boarding-house rooms.

He unlocked a door and showed us into an attic room. Cabbage, curry, plus dirty socks. There was a single bed squashed against the wall where the roof sloped down, and a hot plate, and a sink. The rest of the space was taken by a gigantic train set.

"See here, boys," said Ramsbottom. "Take a look at my Baldwin 4-6-0. It runs on an Arnold chassis, with a Walschaert valve gear. That's a hundred hours' work."

"Good heavens!" Mom exclaimed.

"And d'you know how I'm going to decorate the bridge?"

We shook our heads.

"I'll stick stone-patterned paper on balsa wood, cut it in hundreds of tiny rectangles, and then apply each one individually. With tweezers."

"Well! I'm impressed! How about you, boys?"

"It's a big set," I said. One hundred feet of centipedey track wove around and around, in and out of tunnels, and over bridges.

"There's even a timetable," he whispered confidentially to Mom. He was laying bare his soul.

"Oh, Mr. Ramsbottom, I really wish Bryan would take up an interest like this. Something creative and constructive. It breaks my heart, the way kids nowadays just fritter away their time."

"When there are so many wholesome pursuits open to the young," he agreed. "Stamp collecting, for instance, or bird-watching."

If you ask me, Ramsbottom likes trains because he can control them—unlike children. And it's strange, isn't it, how uninteresting people with interests are? In my opinion there's got to be something wrong with your life if you need interests. Most people just get on with living. Although I do have one little hobby, which I will tell you about later.

Because Miss Glancey was ill, we had religion class on Friday morning after gym. Ramsbottom had just taken us for gym, and we'd solved the mystery of why he shrinks during this class. A quick nose around the changing room had revealed two wedges in his shoes, thick enough to add an inch to his height.

"Can't be good for his feet," said Josh, chucking them down a toilet. "Why, he's practically walking around on tiptoe."

So it was a more than usually flat-footed Ramsbottom who chalked *Transsubstantiation, Transmigration, Reincarnation* on the blackboard.

"Excuse me, sir," I piped up. "I can't see what you've written. It's too low. Could you write it higher?"

The class giggled.

"You could pile up some books," said Josh.

"Or stand on the chair," said someone else.

"Should I ask the janitor for a ladder?" came from the back.

"SILENCE!" Ramsbottom shrieked. "We are here to talk about souls, though it is hard to believe you people have any, and what happens to them when you die. If the Christians prove to be right, Bryan Rignall, you will undoubtedly go to Hell."

We were trying to get a string of bubblegum to stretch all the way across the room by passing it from desk to desk.

"On the other hand," he continued loudly, "the Hindus believe your soul will simply turn up in someone else— 'samsara,' meaning 'what turns around forever.' A chance to do better next time, eh, Joshua? Are you paying attention, Joshua? What did I just say?"

"Something about samosas, sir."

Ramsbottom slapped the book down on the table and rolled up his eyes. "I give up. Read chapter five in the textbook, and write me an essay called 'Life after death.' Next week we'll go train spotting."

I saw him first, waving at the end of the platform, by the snack bar. He was wearing a green parka, a backpack, a cap, and mountaineering boots.

"Going camping, sir?" asked Josh.

"Have we all got notebooks, boys? And pens? Dear me, we've just missed a new design for an intercity train. Never mind. Let's sit down and have our sandwiches."

He seemed quite excited, even though the bar wasn't open yet. He sat on a bench and took a flask from the backpack, and a plastic lunch box.

"Anchovy sandwiches, anybody?" he offered.

"Um . . . no thanks, sir . . . we'll get a hamburger at the cafeteria."

When we came out, an hour later, he was standing by the signal box. He looked surprised to see us.

"Forgotten us, Mr. Ramsbottom?" I said.

"I must say, this outing was a good idea." His specs sparkled. "Look how my notebook's filling up! So much of interest here, isn't there?"

"We're going to do some observation from the bridge," I told him. There's an old-fashioned stone bridge over the mouth of a tunnel. Very picturesque, just like the rest of the station. We got a good view from the top, of the glass roof with its fancy ironwork, and the nicely kept flower-beds at the end. Mr. Ramsbottom was talking to the stationmaster, and they looked just like those little models in the store.

"Okay," said Josh, taking off his backpack. "What colors you got?"

"Red," I said, "and blue. How about you?"

"I've got a really good silver one, and a black." He rummaged around in his gym bag and pulled out a couple of cans. We settled down on the wall, swinging our legs and enjoying the sunshine. Then we shook the cans, waiting for that little ball to start rattling.

"This is the fun part of train spotting," said Josh. "Putting the spots on the trains."

"I'll start," I said. Josh has to admit I am ace at letter-

59

ing. I like doing trains best, but bridges will do. Josh held on to my feet, because it can be dangerous when you're leaning that far over. I got the letters a good yard high, all across the bridge, and when I'd finished we ran down the steps to admire my handiwork. It said:

ЯAWSBOTAW STINᴋS

"Why did you write it in Russian?" taunted Josh. "Rawsbotaw," he read out loud. "It's Chinese."

"I bet you couldn't do it upside down," I protested. He snickered.

"Make a good bumper sticker, wouldn't it? *Graffiti Artists Do It Upside Down.*"

I was considering the bridge. "There's a ledge I could stand on," I said. "If I spray the mistakes in black, then go over in silver, it'll look even better." I'm a real perfectionist.

We went back up and shook the cans again, and then I climbed over the parapet. The ledge was only a few inches deep, so I took off my shoes and socks to get a better grip. My fingers were just curling over the top.

By now we had quite an audience. The whole class was there, in enthralled silence. Old Ramsbottom was still down at the other end, apparently sketching point connections in his notebook. He should get such attention. Anyway, I edged my way along and let go with one hand. Josh put the black paint can in it, and I started to spray over the letters.

That was when the train came through, out of the tunnel. It must have been doing over 100 mph, and I was shocked at the force of it, at the sucking wind. I realized how low I was as tons of shiny metal hurtled beneath me, just a few inches away. I dropped the can, which bounced off the train roof and clattered onto the rails. I shouted to Josh to pull me up, but the rushing, clicketing train ate my words. As the last car left the tunnel, the blast of wind tugged my legs, throwing my weight onto my fingers. I felt them slipping.

Oh, God, I think, this is it. As I fall, I clutch a bracket sticking out of the stonework. Now my legs are hanging over the track, swinging into the tunnel. There's shouting, footsteps, merging in a blur of panic.

"Hang on," someone cries out. Another voice keeps yelling, "Don't touch the power lines, don't touch the power lines, whatever you do." Someone's panting . . . there's a grunt, then I hear shuffling, somewhere near my left ear.

"Well, Bryan, this is a fine mess you've gotten me into!"

I squint up, and see a pair of mountaineering boots on the ledge. A hand reaches down and grasps my wrist. It pulls, firm and strong. It's gonna be all right, I think, realizing I can get one foot on the ledge again.

I'm swinging the other leg up when I hear rumbling. I look over my shoulder. There's a train thundering from the other end of the station. It's got to stop; I need just two seconds and I'll be clear, but it's still coming at me . . . Why is everything in slow motion, apart from that train? . . . If I clutch the hand, a last desperate heave . . .

There's an explosive blow to my leg, and we're both gobbled up by the train and the tunnel, dragged into blackness and pain. Crushing agony grinds my body, and I can't see, there's blood in my nose and mouth, my skull's in a vice of sickening pressure. I don't know who, what, where I am, it's all swirling away like water down the drain. . . . I struggle.

I feel hands pulling, and a cloth gently wiping my face. I open my eyes. They meet eyes below a white mask, a doctor's mask. He's smiling at me.

"It's a boy!" he says, and hands me to a woman lying in bed.

"Isn't he lovely?" she exclaims. "Look at those little tufts of hair. I think I'll call him Richard. Richard Woolias is a fine name, don't you think, Doctor?"

I open my mouth in a toothless scream.

Hunters

At six o'clock, as usual, the Pearces were having their supper. It was a substantial meal—meat pie, peas, carrots, french fries—because they worked hard and needed to keep up their strength. Although they were farmers, the meal was made from frozen food to save time.

"They tell me, down the village, they seen the old fox prowlin' around our top field," said Edna challengingly.

Leonard poured ketchup on his fries but said nothing.

"He'll be in at the chickens again, mark my words, unless you do something," she insisted.

Leonard reached for the newspaper and grunted. "He'll never get in the coop since I fixed it. Beautiful beast like that, I don't wish it no harm."

"You're soft, you," she said. "It's always me, isn't it, doin' the dirty work?" She swallowed the last of her coffee and pushed back her chair.

At six o'clock, as usual, the Mercers were having their supper. Today it was steamed vegetables and baked potatoes, fresh farm produce, healthy for growing children.

"Oh, come on, Dad," Keith was saying. "It's only two miles, and I am thirteen now. My bike's got reflectors and lights. It's only lanes, not busy roads, and you can always hear a car coming when it's miles away."

"I suppose the whole point of Scouts is to teach them independence," said Mrs. Mercer, "and he's a good boy, on the whole. Sensible, you must admit."

"Well . . ."

"You've got to let me out by myself sooner or later."

"Tell you what, then. You call us when you get there, and we'll come at eight to pick you up. How's that?"

"Old worrywart!" said Keith fondly.

Edna Pearce went onto the porch and pulled on her boots and fingerless woolen gloves. As she closed the door, the sun fell on her face and shoulders; her body and the farm-yard were submerged in the blue evening, deep as a swimming pool. She clicked her tongue at the chickens, rounding them up, then carried the feed bucket to the henhouse. Stooping, she spread grain along the trough. As she backed out of the stinking din and straightened to fasten the door, she gazed past the cow shed and up the hill. Shadows from the hunched woods rolled far down the field; another day ending, another year. Seemed pointless sometimes, working so hard to keep the farm with no child to pass it on to.

She put her hand up to shade her eyes and saw something, a dog perhaps, running diagonally up the higher field, leaping over the ridges.

Keith Mercer wheeled his bike out of the garage. He climbed on and freewheeled down the driveway. At the gate he looked carefully in both directions before turning onto the road. Although the sun was only just behind the roofs, he had his lights on. His bicycle was polished, his uniform was clean and pressed. Keith liked order.

He leaned forward, putting his weight on the pedals, and the bicycle labored up the hill. At the top the pavement suddenly blazed, and he sped gloriously over into the sunset. He flew past houses in pairs like married couples, each with its own little car tucked in for the night in its own little garage, flew past the yards along the winding roads. The hedges were tall, so he pinged his bell at every bend. He loved the sight of his knuckles on the black molded rubber, the glittering handlebars with the round bell; he loved the power of his own legs propelling him away.

A tractor trundled down the next hill toward him, so he steered into the cow parsley at the side of the road. He got off, and the driver nodded at him. "Evenin'," he called as he drove past. Keith pushed the bike toward the road again, then swore; there was a patch of nettles he hadn't noticed, and because of the Scouting shorts, his legs were bare. He pushed the bike a little farther up the road, leaned it against a gate, and looked around for some dock leaves to rub onto the rash. According to the Scout manual you can always find dock leaves where there are nettles, he thought.

Edna ran across the yard to the porch, skidding on the manure. She seized the shotgun from behind the door and

65

the satchel with the cartridges, and slinging them over her shoulder, yelled, "I think I saw him, Len. The fox! You comin'?"

A snore drifted back from the kitchen. She crossed the yard at a trot, and through the gate, closing it after her. The hill was steep, and as she slowed to a walk, she lifted the gun into position to load the cartridges. She adjusted the safety catch and rested the gun on her shoulder. At the elm tree she stopped to catch her breath. Peering around it, she could find no sign of the fox. Perhaps he'd seen her coming and had run into the woods. Shouldn't have got into such a frenzy; should have taken it slow, she told herself sternly. Not to worry—it was probably just a dog, anyway.

Then she saw him. About thirty feet away, standing stockstill, in profile. He was watching something, not her; he hadn't seen her. Vicious brute, she thought, remembering her leghorns strewn all around the coop in a snowstorm of feathers. The fox hadn't even eaten the chickens; he'd just played with them. No point in bein' sentimental, she thought. Cruel, that's what nature's ways are; pointless and cruel.

She lifted the shotgun and quietly released the safety catch. As she squinted down the barrel and swung the sights level with his head, the fox abruptly bounded forward, zigzagging through the grass. In a second he was behind the hedge.

"Sukebind, chicory, bogwort, sedge," recited Keith, as he searched among the bushes. One thing about the Scouts, they sure teach you a lot about nature. And there it was, a big clump of dock leaves under a hawthorn bush. He tugged a few leaves out and climbed over the stile by the gate. Then he settled himself comfortably on the step and rubbed the leaves up and down on his shins. Either it really works, he thought, or you think it does, which comes to the same thing. Or by the time you've found the dock leaves, it's stopped hurting anyway.

He looked around the field at the red-tipped grass, the trees clotted black against sky like streaky bacon; it was all unnaturally sharp, bright as a vision. He glanced at his watch. Six-forty. Got to go now, or I'll be late, he thought reluctantly. They rely on me to help with the little kids. He saw a rabbit, happily ambling along by the hedge on his left. Every now and then it stopped for a nibble; then its tail would pop up as it bobbed on through the goose grass.

Keith watched, not moving a muscle so he wouldn't scare it. Every hair shone positively silver, and its eyes were moist and dark as elderberries. Then he caught his breath, for unbelievably, even better, there was a fox farther up the field. The fox was watching the rabbit too; his ears were pricked in concentration, and he crouched low. Gradually he began to glide forward, so smoothly that his body appeared to float over the grass.

All at once the rabbit was weaving through the undergrowth. The fox shot after it, but skidded to a halt as it vanished into the hedge. He stood, head forward and swinging, sniffing the air.

Of course, thought Keith, that's why he hasn't noticed me. I'm upwind. He can't smell me. He remembered that his camera was in the saddlebag. Very slowly he leaned

67

over and fumbled in the bag till he found it. Funny, he thought, I'm watching the fox, who's watching the rabbit, who's watching something else. We're all, like, hunters—it's a chain of command, sort of, with me on top. Well ordered, that's Mother Nature. He peered through the viewfinder, but was disappointed to see how far away the fox appeared. He tried to recollect the tracking techniques he'd learned at Scouts. If I get behind the brambles, he thought, and creep along right beside the hedge, I should be able to get really close.

This is crazy, thought Edna, coming out from behind the elm. Tearing around the fields at my age. What hope is there of my catchin' a fox! Much chance as a snowball in hell. He's crafty as a human—and a darn sight faster. She lit a cigarette and began to trudge up toward the hedge. I'll just take a little peep over, though I'll bet he's gone by now. Lifting her boots carefully so as not to squelch in the damp patches, she glanced back. Down in the valley the farm lights glowed in the dusk. Hope Len's woke up for the milkin', she thought.

The grass was muddier than Keith, on hands and knees, had bargained for. At least he hoped it was mud; this field was usually full of cows. Brambles scratched him and smeared his clothes with blackberry juice until he decided to turn back. After all, by now there was scarcely enough light for a photo, and the Scoutmaster would be wondering what had happened to him; but then, through a gap in the leaves, he saw the fox again.

Its fur was crimson in the setting sun, rippling in the

breeze. As for the eyes, they were green slits so purely wild that he was humbled. For an instant he saw himself as the fox might see him—crouched in the mud with his bottom in the air, in his silly uniform, with a silly lump of black metal swinging from his neck. Then he edged forward.

There was something behind the hawthorn hedge, Edna was sure of it. She dropped the cigarette and ground it absentmindedly with her heel as she peered into the foliage. Although the hedge was thick, she could definitely make out a shadow creeping beyond it. Occasionally fronds at the top fluttered as whatever it was brushed the branches below. It must be the fox. She leveled the shotgun against her shoulder and squinted down the barrel at the moving shape, following it. She squeezed the trigger.

It was six-fifty when the sun finally sank behind the woods; a rabbit, a fox, and a cacophony of crows followed it, as the crack of the gun echoed around and around the darkening valley.

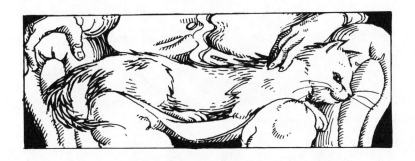

The Takeover

The honey-colored cat was on the doorstep again. As soon as he saw the woman, he began to purr, rubbing himself against her legs. She bent to stroke him.

"Look out, sweetie," she crooned as he twined around her ankles. "We don't want to fall and break a hip, do we?" She put down a shopping bag and dug around in her pocket for the door key. As he gazed up at her, she admired his fluffiness, his sweet face with those breathtaking amber eyes. He was like the teddy bears in the commercials, but living and breathing, loving as well as lovable. The cat sprang onto the wall and watched her arthritic fumblings as she let herself in.

"It's no use hanging around here," she told him. "My pension wouldn't keep a mouse, let alone a great tiger like you. Scat now."

The cat's eyes narrowed humorously as she picked up her shopping and closed the door. He stretched out along the wall and lay quite still, apart from one ear swiveling like a radar dish. He was in no hurry.

The next morning the old lady slopped into the kitchen, slippers flapping, hair unraveled. She lifted the kettle, assessing whether it held enough water for one cup of coffee, and carried it to the sink. As she held it under the tap, a shadow fell across her hands.

"Not you again!" she exclaimed, seeing the silhouette at the window. She huffed, then sighed. "Oh, all right, just this once. Come on. I've got some leftovers somewhere. But don't think you can make a habit of this!"

She wrestled with the rusty catch and pushed the window open a crack. The cat oozed in. He sniffed around the kitchen, printing tracks like bruises across the linoleum before turning to the food. Then he followed the woman into the living room and settled himself on the back of her armchair, where there was a view of the garden. His eyes smiled with all the confidence of a perfect being as his body languorously extended.

"Diddums puss-puss like some milkies? Mommy's sweet boy want milkums?"

He ignored her and began to groom himself, licking every inch. He was efficient and economical in his movements, extending a leg over his shoulder as he worked along his tail, then licking a paw to clean the ears. His fur glowed like a flame in the dim room, emphasizing its drabness.

"What are you thinking, darlin'? I wonder what goes on in that pretty little head. Not a lot, I guess."

The cat tucked in his limbs tidily and turned his attention to the giant who'd given him shelter.

"You're all charm, aren't you? Got a built-in smile," the

giant said. She switched on the box in the corner, a black box with one bright wall, and sank into her armchair in front of it. The box seemed to suck up the world of giants and make it small, like a sort of waste disposal machine. At tumultuous speed all their chaos and ugliness flickered around the cube. Every now and then the noise swelled.

"See our Georgian security lamps . . ."

"Now, how about them, puss-puss. They look really useful."

". . . installed on your patio, will welcome friends, deter intruders!"

"On second thought, kitten, with my luck they'd work the other way around. Can't be too careful, can we?" She scratched him under the chin.

"Special offer on our Rodeo Barbecue, with accessories," the box burbled on. "Get your garden chairs and cocktail carts from Outa-Doors Garden Centers NOW!"

The cat surveyed the garden. It was wild, as overgrown as nature intended, but that was good; leaves and flowers swayed in subtle rhythms, all was harmoniously alive, and he was master. For him it was a 3-D military map, and chirrups in the warm air placed each bird with the precision of a flagged pin. His general's whiskers twitched. This world was not the world of giants, where the hard things they made became jagged and rusty but would not die, and the giants wrinkled and grew useless but would not die.

"It's nearly midnight, fluffikins. We must be getting our beauty sleep," said the giant. "I'll leave the kitchen window open for you, but no yowling on the garbage cans, okay?"

It switched off the cube and shuffled away carrying the milk bottles. The cat uncurled and jumped onto the floor. He stretched, paws and head low, tail high over curving back. Then he sat up and listened.

Bottles clink. Steps slur down the hall. The front door opens and closes. Steps up the stairs. Another door. Rushing water. Footsteps. Door. Silence . . . silence.

The cat is fully alert now, neck outstretched and ears pricked. He waits a little longer. Then, as the church clock begins to strike twelve, he slips through the window and leaps high onto the garden wall.

He looks around, and the vertical black slits in his eyes eclipse the gold. On every wall, as far as he can see, are the outlines of other cats. Ten, fifty, a hundred cats, multiplying in every direction. A thousand cats, poised on roofs and garbage cans, on sheds and steps and branches, a million cats, waiting, listening. The clock tolls like a giant heart, and as it strikes its final beat, they are gathered. The last unit has been infiltrated; this night, when every house in the world has a cat, is the night of the takeover.

Like parts of a single powerful beast, the cats silently and simultaneously vanish into the dark. The honey-colored cat creeps back into the kitchen, delicately pads around the sink, and jumps to the floor. His back arches, and he seems larger as the fur bristles along his spine. He looks at the moon and slides a pointed tongue around his teeth; they gleam, stars flashing from their sharp points. He turns and slinks into the dim hall. Then, soft as a shadow, he ripples up the stairs to do what must be done.

Chain Letter

The Valley of Naukratis
5th September 1908

I t was I who found it, this I swear to God. Lord Meryon will doubtless take the glory and wealth that are mine by right; no matter. I had been searching the valley for nearly twelve years, when less than two months ago I came upon the tomb. It was at the north end, near a wasteland of sour grass grazed by goats. The only clue was a low mound, about twenty feet long, where my light digging turned up some fragments of pottery. A little farther down, I came across smooth stone. When I brushed the loose sand away with my fingers, my eyes met a carved eye, slanting away to a cruelly curved beak. The thrill was indescribable; I knew that this was a statue of the god Namon Ra, and that I had found the tomb of Pharaoh Ramhotep III, his disciple.

I hurried back to Cairo, where I telegraphed the news to Lord Meryon. It was vital that he should help me; he had money and influence, whereas I had only a meager allowance from my uncle. Meryon came, within a week, bringing men. The *fellahin* were reluctant, fearing the god, but Meryon paid them well. What justice is there when such a well-born man has also wealth, wit, and a handsome face? All I had to make my way in the world was ambition.

Nevertheless, I admit I was delighted to see him. It was dusk on the twentieth of July; I had been sitting in the shadow of my tent watching the sky turn the color of good burgundy, when I noticed a froth of dust on the horizon. An hour later a line of horsemen came out of the palm trees to the east. I leaped to my feet, throwing my hat into the air, and ran to meet them. My friend Henry Meryon (for then he was still my friend) jumped from his horse as he saw me and ran to shake my hand.

"Jack, my dear fellow, this is a momentous occasion. We must start the dig at first light tomorrow. And I have a surprise for you—who do you think is with us?"

I looked along the line of horses and among the skirts of the *bedouin* saw the riding habit of an Englishwoman. My heart bounded.

"Could it be Ellen?" I asked, hardly daring to hope.

"Indeed, risking mosquitoes and sunburn just to see you. But as we need help with the cataloguing . . ."

I swung her from the horse and lifted the veil of her hat to kiss her. "You shouldn't have come, my dear. This is no place for a woman."

"Heroines are going everywhere nowadays, Jack, didn't you know? The best method of restraint is chaining 'em to railway lines," Meryon interrupted, "but this one got away. Put the poor girl down—she's hot enough already."

"Henry and Ellen," I said, putting an arm around each waist, "my two dearest friends, until the bearers have made camp, you must come to my tent and have a good cup of Indian tea. I can only apologize for the goat's milk."

I believe that evening was the happiest of my life. We sat and talked the night away, and our hopes were as long as our shadows across the sand.

By five o'clock the next morning our company was ready to start work; the bedouin were as curious as we were to uncover the statue and find what lay beneath. It took several hours to free Namon Ra from the sand, and it was an awesome sight when he finally surfaced, like a drowned man rising from the depths. Standing, he would have been forty feet tall; but now his giant wings lay flat on the desert, his eyes gazed blindly at the sky. Meryon stood as if turned to stone himself, but I was impatient.

"Look at that loose masonry, Henry. We must put the men to work there. It could well be the entrance to the tomb."

"Don't gods impress you, Jack?"

"You may stand there till the sands cover your head, if you wish, but remember what you are paying these twenty men; set them to it."

The sun was growing oppressively hot, and I knew we'd be able to dig for only a few more hours. I worked them hard, and I worked with them, shoulder to sweating shoulder. The dunes rang to the thrust of spades, as Meryon sat with Ellen on the chest of the stone god and held her parasol for her; they might have been having tea at Twickenham. I was in good spirits, however, as we soon uncovered a flight of rock-hewn steps that reached down some thirty feet, leading to a sloping passage.

We worked for several days, until the passage turned to another staircase, flanked by shelves. These were empty but for a bundle of ancient onions. A few yards farther we found a wall plastered with mud and sealed with the priestly seal. I pushed the men aside and grabbed a chisel.

"Fetch Lord Meryon at once," I ordered, and began to hack furiously at the wall. It instantly fractured, and I dragged out the bricks with all my strength until my hands bled.

"Give me a candle," I shouted over my shoulder. "Hurry, you fools, must I wait all day?" Enough light sifted through the dust for me to see a confusion of dark forms, glittering with the occasional touch of gold or silver. I squeezed through the hole and dropped into the chamber. A boy handed me a lighted candle, and I looked around, beside myself with excitement.

"Are you there, Jack? Are you all right?"

Meryon was blocking the daylight.

"For heaven's sake, man, get out of the way. Ask the boy for more candles and climb down."

We were overwhelmed by the beauty before us. Gradually one object after another swam free of the shimmering mass and shone through the cool air, dust free and golden. The room was about a hundred feet long, and carved from the solid rock. Around us were couches, chairs, and alabaster vases, bedecked with precious stones. I saw lapis lazuli, turquoise, carnelian, obsidian, and faience, all exquisitely worked and designed. None shone brighter, though, in the fluttering candlelight, than Meryon's eyes.

They met mine, but we did not speak. Along the left wall a row of harps presided proudly over some small skeletons; Ramhotep must have wanted his maiden harpists with him. Similarly, against the other wall was a row of magnificent chariots, with the gruesome remains of their drivers. I shivered.

"What better proof that greed is folly?" I murmured. "We all return to dust."

"But our possessions do not, and the beauty we leave behind." Meryon's hands were trembling. "What a glorious memorial to leave for future generations."

"There is precious little glory in having your grave robbed by two low scoundrels," I laughed.

"*You* may be a low scoundrel, Jack . . ."

His cousin is King Edward, as he is fond of reminding me.

"As one who's so intimate with royalty," I rejoined, "perhaps you can direct me to the pharaoh? There's no sarcophagus here."

"It must be in a farther chamber; d'you see that far wall?"

We made our way through the room and found at the end a bricked-up doorway guarded by two statues, each bearing on its forehead a vulture and a cobra. I took the chisel and hammer from my pocket and set vigorously to work.

"Have a little respect, Jack. You're noisy enough to wake the dead!"

"The day I see you wielding anything heavier than a croquet mallet will be the day you may criticize my labor," I retorted, rubble piling about my feet. "Until then, make yourself useful and find a pail."

"But you're through! Move that large slab and we'll be able to see."

I stuck my hand, with the candle, through the hole, and wriggled my shoulder and head after it. To my disappointment, the chamber was small and practically empty. There was just a gilded chariot yoke, a scarab, and a slender, long green staff circled with gilding near the top.

"It looks as if thieves have been here before us," I said, withdrawing so that Meryon could look.

"But if that was so, why haven't they robbed the outer chamber? It's very odd. And very disappointing." He put down the candle and brushed the plaster from his white flannel trousers.

"Henry, haven't we wonders enough to amaze the world? But first I want to share this moment with Ellen. Then we must tackle the mighty task of cataloguing the treasures and arranging their transport to England."

The work of excavation was nothing compared to the work of removal.

"You're as fussy as a Kensington housewife," complained Meryon. "Will you ever be finished with your feather duster, so that we can get back to civilization?"

"This *is* civilization, you simple fellow. The grouse season must do without you for once. And doesn't it occur to you that we might get along much faster if you lent a hand?"

"Those dry corpses with open eyes are enough to give a man the horrors. You're less sensitive than I, Jack, and never happier than when getting your hands dirty, like a child making mud pies. So stick at it, my boy, and I'll help Ellen with the catalogue. Tedious though it may be."

I indulged his indolence—I wanted his wealth to be the ladder out of my pit of poverty and obscurity—so I have only myself to blame for the turn of events.

It was this very morning that those events inexorably began. I was working with the fellahin to clear the last items from the tomb. After a time we took a rest, drinking from leather bottles. I lay back against the smooth flank of Namon Ra and watched the undulating heat haze; I was relaxed and cheerful, feeling the satisfaction of achievement. Tomorrow we would set off for England, where success and fame would also be mine. And Ellen, dearest Ellen, after all these years would be mine. As I daydreamed, I realized that the bedouin had moved away and were speaking excitedly. I strained my ears, trying to understand the dialect.

"It is only a rumor, passed on from my grandfather's uncle."

"But what if it is true? We must wait until the *effendis* have gone and take the spoils to divide among ourselves. We will be rich men."

"Don't be so foolish, boy. Do you not know that the pharaohs had two precautions against looters? One is, as I have just told you, to build a false burial room to mislead ignorant robbers; the other, my grandfather says, was to lay a curse on him who enters the true tomb. Would you risk the wrath of Namon Ra?"

They noticed I was watching them, and lowered their voices. What they are saying, I told myself, is that there is a concealed burial chamber down there, just waiting to be discovered, which might hold even greater treasure! I closed my eyes, pretending to sleep for a while; if they'd known I'd understood their superstitious nonsense, they might have abandoned the packing.

"I shall go back to camp to see if the crates are ready," I said when we had resumed work. I had to tell Meryon and Ellen what I had heard, and when I reached the tamarisk trees, I began to run. I felt as if I could fly. This would be the only complete and unpillaged tomb ever discovered, belonging to the richest pharaoh of them all. And I, Jack Wells, had found it!

I slowed down, fighting to get my breath back, as I saw my friends sitting at the table, numbering amphorae. Their heads were close together.

"You'll have to tell him soon," said Meryon. "We're leaving tomorrow."

"I know, Henry. You don't have to remind me. It's just not that easy. He's waited all these years for me; it'll break his heart."

I drew back behind the tent. Suddenly I felt cold.

"You're too compassionate, my dearest," Meryon continued. "He loves these old relics more than you. And you know he's as happy as a sandboy grubbing in the dirt; he'll soon get over it."

"But I was fond of him; I still am."

He took her hand and clasped it. "I'm fond of him too; funny old fellow, with his smiling red face and violent enthusiasms. But you deserve a finer life than he can offer you. I can make you happy—you'll see."

Grief and fury warred in my breast. I slunk away into the trees, then sank to my knees and wept.

At noon I returned to the tomb, bringing with me the men's wages. The fellahin had already sent the treasures off to Cairo, so I paid them and bade them farewell.

I ran through the stairways and corridors to the large chamber and began to tap my way around the walls. Halfway along the west side there was a niche, holding a sacrificial skull and three legs of a bull. Behind them the wall sounded hollow. I struck again and again with my chisel until a hole formed.

There, before my eyes, was the burial chamber of Ramhotep III, in all its glory—an unimaginable treasure trove. And I tell you, it was nothing to me, so much gaudy trash; but it would serve my purpose. I prepared my materials and went to the camp. By good fortune Ellen was not to be seen.

"Henry!" I called jovially. "We need a little help. Do you think you could stir yourself?"

"You're a slave driver, Jack. Wouldn't you like a cool drink? You look quite purple."

"Come along, now, your lordship. You know the ship sails tomorrow and won't wait, even for you."

I led him over the burning sand and into the entrails of the earth.

"See what I've found, Henry. This'll make 'em sit up at the British Museum."

He looked into the hole, his mouth a perfect circle.

"Get in, take a look, why don't you?" I helped him through and handed him a candle. He stared at me, puzzled.

"You're looking very peculiar, old chap. Is it a touch of the sun?"

85

"No, 'old chap,' it's a touch of disloyalty, a touch of betrayal. A touch of base, underhanded treachery. But you aren't going to get away with it. I'm going to wall you up here with your good friend Ramhotep, and you may enjoy his royal company for eternity."

He laughed nervously.

"But the men will be back soon."

"I've paid them off. Their work is finished."

I spread the mortar with a steady hand and laid the heavy slabs.

"What about Ellen? She'll organize a search party."

"My dear Henry, I shall organize a search party; but by the time it gets here, you will be suffocated and the plaster will be dry. Never mind, future generations will still be able to admire the beauties of your fine country house."

His fingers kept scrabbling at the bricks as I laid them. A smart tap with my hammer soon put a stop to that. He said no more, and the wall proceeded well. I was six inches from the top when suddenly his arm shot through the hole, and grabbed my collar. He twisted it with a savagery and strength I had not known him capable of. I was choking, my veins swelling in agony. I writhed, striking out with the trowel. Silently we fought for our lives. As I pushed my knee against the wall, I heard a crack; it had split from floor to ceiling, and bricks came tumbling all around me. The wall fell, and Meryon, coughing from the dust, sprang out. I did not care that each moment might be my last—I was determined the blackguard should not escape. We struggled in the dirt, with the tomb crumbling over our heads. He managed to get to his feet, then kicked me in the stomach and ran for the stairs. I saw his shape against the light; then it was gone. I was on my back. Above me cracks forked across the ceiling like lightning. The very rock had split asunder, was caving in. I crawled toward the burial chamber that held firm as, with a roar like the laughter of the gods, the outer sanctum collapsed.

I crouched with my head in my arms. I have never felt such terror. When the tumult ebbed, I looked up and saw that I was entombed.

By some miracle, Meryon's candle still stands. I am at the feet of Prince Ramhotep. At his head is another statue of Namon Ra, whose profile casts a shuddering shadow high up the wall. I see ruefully how well provided we are, his Highness and I. There is a great jeweled water jar, and over thirty granite boxes of mummified legs of mutton, duck, and venison. When I touch some, they turn to black powder. There are roses too, transparent as butterflies' wings. By the prince's head is a writing table, complete with papyrus and goose quills. The ink, of course, has dried, but in my pocket is my fountain pen.

Now I have written my testament, that you may know the truth. I have done wrong, but no greater than the wrong that was done to me. And so to my final task, my legacy to you, my dear reader—all I have to bequeath. I have read the hieroglyphics on this parchment. Have you? Did you understand them? Then allow me to translate:

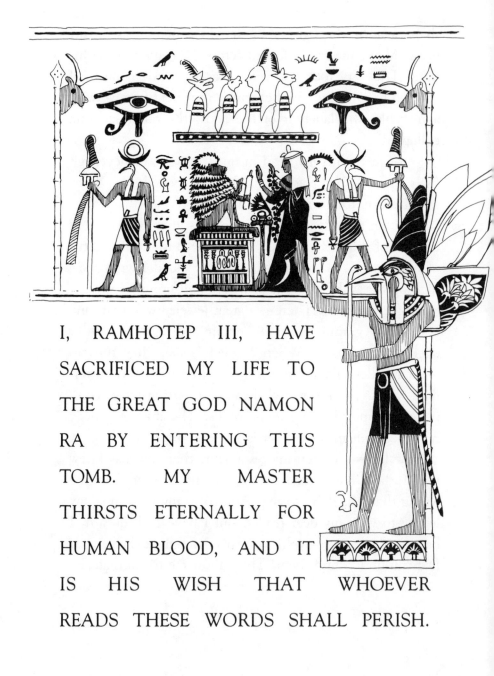

I, RAMHOTEP III, HAVE SACRIFICED MY LIFE TO THE GREAT GOD NAMON RA BY ENTERING THIS TOMB. MY MASTER THIRSTS ETERNALLY FOR HUMAN BLOOD, AND IT IS HIS WISH THAT WHOEVER READS THESE WORDS SHALL PERISH.

My hand leaves dark patches on the papyrus. I can hardly breathe. I tear off my shirt, and sweat trickles down my chest. The candle is guttering, the flame going blue. Soon the air will be gone. My life is draining away, like sand through an hourglass. It is some consolation to me to know that yours is too.

For you must by now have realized that you are the next victim of Namon Ra. Watch out, as you walk down the street, for the shadow of his wings across your sunny path. And when dusk falls, shun the lonely yards and alleys it shrouds most deeply; hasten home, I tell you.

Are you there now? Lock the door, if you will, and bolt it, though iron is as straw to ancient powers. But wait . . . listen! What is it that rustles behind you, that creaks in stealthy tread? Do you feel a chill breath stir the hairs upon your neck?

I wish you better luck than I have had.

Farewell

Video Nasty

Good grief, haven't you taken this back yet?" Scott's father pulled a video cassette from the pile by the television. "You got this on Sunday. They'll fine us a fortune."

"But I did take it back—I'm sure I did. Look, the box isn't there."

"The video is though, isn't it? You must have taken one of ours back. Well, I'm not paying."

"But Dad, that's a whole week's paper-route money!"

"Tough. You shouldn't be so careless."

Scott took the video and went out, slamming the door. It was gray outside—dull pavements, houses all the same, with windows like TV screens giving glimpses of lives as stale as his own, just boring, endless soap operas.

Every morning when he went to school, he walked down this street, and always, halfway down, passed the fat woman with the little girl; on the corner he would cross at the same time as the man in overalls, and coming to Merton Road, he'd see the business lady, then the boy with the backpack. These blank faces day after day were like zombies from *Invasion of the Body Snatchers*. Don't they know we're just cogs, going around and around like clockwork? thought Scott. There must be more to life.

When he reached the main street, he pressed the button at the crossing. The oncoming traffic slowed at his command, a towering tidal wave of cars and trucks holding back for Scott, like Moses, to cross. He ran the last few yards to the video shop and shuffled his feet through the swirling rubbish to look in the window. It was the only window on the street that wasn't broken or boarded up. And what a window! It was packed with posters offering excitement and adventure, and despite himself his heart lifted as he looked at them. There were, roughly speaking, two kinds of posters: soft ones, with dissolving flesh, sliding eyeballs, and titles that dribbled blood; and hard ones, with hard shiny men and their hard shiny cars and guns. Scott liked the second kind best.

Release date June 5th, he read. *RAW GUN III. Lieutenant Jeff Storm has the toughest unit in the Delta. He must prove himself in battle where one mistake means death. The final test comes in a brutal rampage of destruction, a terrifying nightmare of bloody vengeance. Rated R.*

Scott pushed open the door and went in. He loved the sense of being grown-up, of being a man, that the video shop gave him. It was like a pool hall or a bar, only better. You could hardly breathe because of cigarette smoke. There was a German shepherd dozing on the counter while the owner discussed with a customer the relative merits of *Convent Girls* and *Snow White and the Seven Dwarfs*.

From the back room, a den of alluring squalor, came

91

the assistant. He was a young man who had weight trained to such an extent that his arms stuck out sideways. Scott wondered how he managed his buttons.

"What number?"

"It's 1802. Martindale."

The youth tapped the number into the computer.

"That'll be twenty dollars."

"No, you see, what happened was I brought back one of our videos by mistake," begged Scott.

"That makes no difference to us, does it? If another customer wants the video, it's money out of our pockets."

"Hey," said the owner, "don't bully the boy, Regis. He's a regular. Should I take a look under the counter, Scott, see what I can find?" He winked. "This is where we keep all the good stuff. Pirated tapes, import specials, you name it. Not to any members of the police force, though!" He laughed. "Hello hello hello! What do you suppose this is?" He spun a black box across the counter. "Scott Martindale," he announced. "This Is Your Life!"

The box was labeled HOME MOVIES. Scott felt a deep blush spreading from his toes to his fingertips.

"We been watching this out back," said Regis. "Your life flashed before our eyes. Ever thought of going in for acting, Scott?"

"Don't tease, now, Reggie. Here you are, son. Take care."

When he got back, his mother was in the living room having a cup of coffee with a friend.

"Hello, dear. Where did you go off to?"

"I had to get this from the video shop."

"I wish you wouldn't go there, Scott. That place really gives me the willies."

She took the tape. "Hey, I thought we'd erased this. Jackie, you must see this before you go. Come on, Scott, put it on for us."

Scott sighed. "Why do you have to embarrass me?"

"Oh, go on. Put it on."

Even Scott got interested as they watched the baby who used to be him kicking its little legs in the air.

"Oooh!" exclaimed Jackie. "Sweet!"

Then they saw a toddler learning to walk, his face a round version of Scott's with the same dimple in the chin, the same lock of brown hair flopping over his eye. And there was Scott learning to ride a bike, with scabs on his knees, legs suddenly doubled in length. It was magic.

All at once they were watching a wedding.

"How did that get on there?" demanded his mother. "We haven't been to a wedding in ten years."

"Nice to dream, though, isn't it?" said Jackie. "She's a lovely girl. Wish I'd had a dress like that. Say, don't you think the groom looks a little like your Scott? Anyway, I'd better be making tracks." She grabbed for her handbag. " 'Bye, Scott."

His mother went with her friend to the door, and Scott reached out to turn off the video. As his finger touched the button, he noticed a familiar face at the wedding. The camera panned away, and it was gone. He rewound the film a little. There was that face again, a woman, about fifty, dabbing at her eyes with a handkerchief. As she looked up, she smiled, then blew her nose. Scott recognized his mother.

94

There were voices in the hall as the front door closed. His father was home again, and Scott heard both his parents going into the kitchen.

"Come here a minute," he yelled.

"No, you come here. Lost the use of your legs?"

Scott looked back at the screen. Yes, there were his mother and his father, and his uncle Peter, all looking strange. Most of Dad's hair was gone, and he looked tired, with bags under his eyes. And Pete, well, he was so fat his collar wouldn't fasten. But the weirdest thing of all was the bridegroom. What a handsome young guy he was, with a dimple in his chin and a careless lock of hair over one eye! He must be well over six feet tall, bending his head to kiss the bride. Scott was mesmerized. That's me, he thought, in ten, fifteen years' time. He was scared, but he couldn't stop watching.

The scene changed. The young man was sitting by a hospital bed. Oh God, it must be Mom or Dad dying, thought Scott. The camera focused on the pillow. It was the girl, sitting up, her hair loose around her shoulders. She was holding a baby. She passed it to the young man, who smiled and lifted it toward the camera. The scene faded.

Now the girl was standing by the sea, the child, about a year older, leaning from her hip. She was waving. The camera panned to a ship, where a line of men stood high up on the deck; it was moving away from a pier. There were flags and balloons everywhere. The camera zoomed in on the faces at the rail, and among them Scott saw his own. He looked terrific in that army uniform, as good as anything in a video poster. If this is my life, he thought, it's not going to be so bad after all.

A television appeared within the television. "It is now six months," said an announcer, "since the ship *Valiant*, bearing a peacekeeping force, sailed for the Gulf of Tabuk. The Twenty-third Division is still patroling the streets of Abu J'alon in an attempt to control the so-called People's Army. A curfew has been imposed."

Scott was feeling slightly sick. Probably the effect of all that hand-held camera, he thought, but he still couldn't tear his eyes away. They were showing the streets of the city, where ugly modern buildings were made uglier by shell holes. The only cars were burned out, and there were barricades of sandbags topped with barbed wire. The city was shimmering in the heat, so hot that he seemed to be looking through molten glass; so hot that he could almost feel it, could almost smell the dust and sweat and gas.

A jeep came bumping down a cobbled alley, and Scott saw soldiers sprawling in the back of it. The camera closed in on a man leaning against the tailgate. His face was one Scott saw in the mirror every day, only longer, with thick eyebrows and a stubbled chin. The skin was sunburned, the nose peeling. Resting loosely on the man's knees was a rifle. That's an M60, he thought excitedly. Wow! The man looked bored.

"Don't suppose there's any chance of a beer tonight?" he said.

"Not a prayer, buddy."

"Well, let's see how quick we can clean up the old west quarter," said another. "Go through it like a dose of Ex-Lax, blow the little bastards out of their holes."

"I'll vote for that. Then we could try to get down to

the bars—to see where the prettiest girls are," said the soldier who was Scott. The others whistled. The man lit a cigarette and offered the pack around. He sucked hard on his own, holding it between thumb and forefinger and creasing his eyes against the smoke. He was gazing absently down the road. "Ever get the feeling you've been somewhere before when you know you haven't?"

"That's what they call *déjà vu*," answered someone. "It's just a trick of the mind."

The jeep swerved around into a square of shuttered shops, all featureless in the black shadow. Suddenly several young men with machine guns flashed across the square and into a side road. The jeep accelerated across the cobbles. As it careered around the corner, there was a glimpse of flying heels; then the men vanished as fast as they'd appeared.

"Where the hell did they get to?" asked the soldier as the jeep slowed to a crawl.

"They're n—"

There was a crackle of gunfire, and the jeep lurched.

"A tire's blown."

"It's a trap—they led us here."

"No sweat. The other fellas'll pick us up."

A rattle of machine-gun bullets raised spurts of dust along the road, and the men leaped from the jeep. At the same time Scott slid from the sofa. Without taking his eyes from the screen, he shuffled closer to the television and sat crouched with his arms around his knees, rocking back and forth.

"It's a rabbit warren in there—we'll never catch 'em," one of the soldiers cried out as they backed against a wall.

97

"The way you catch rabbits is smoke 'em out," said another.

"That's right," said the soldier Scott. "Let's have some fireworks, a little fun."

He kicked a door in, and the camera looked through a passage to a courtyard. There were women peeling vegetables, chattering, with hens and children around their feet. At once their faces paled with fear.

"Where are they?" shouted the soldier, running into the yard. He was holding a grenade. The women grabbed the children and scattered to the nearest doorways. A tray fell to the ground, rolling lazily away through the red and yellow peppers in the dirt. A mother ran for the last child, her robed arms swooping like protective wings, as the man tugged out the pin and hurled the grenade. There was a flash and a roar. When the dust cleared, Scott saw two bodies in the yard, one already shrouded in black, the other with bare limbs sprawled open to the sky. The child's mouth was open, as were his eyes, which stared at the sun. It was snowing chicken feathers, and they drifted softly over his skin, sticking where there was blood. In the house someone moaned.

Tears trickled down Scott's cheeks, and he rubbed his sleeve across his eyes to clear them. He wanted to turn it off, but he had to know what would happen. Then machine-gun fire came again from high on a white church tower, and the soldiers backed down the passage, reloading their guns. Scott dragged himself up and grabbed the sides of the television as if it was a person he wanted to shake. He screamed, a shriek sharp enough to pierce time.

"Stop, it's wrong; you can't do this!"

The man hesitated. He looked back into the yard with a puzzled expression, as if there was something he must remember at all costs. He frowned, chewing his lip, then wiped a sweaty hand on his shirt and turned to leave. It was too late; his way was barred by a guerrilla with a raised revolver.

Scott heard the door open. He swiveled and saw his father's surprised face peering around it. "What the heck's all the racket about?" he complained. Scott slumped onto the carpet. He didn't answer but looked back to the screen, where the soldier knelt before the guerrilla, the revolver pressed against his forehead. The picture swelled into close-up, and Scott could see that the soldier was whimpering, sweat cutting runnels through the dirt on his face. His eyelids were closed, the lashes fluttering as the guerrilla grasped his hair. His hands rose ineffectually.

The guerrilla tugged the man's head back, and his finger tightened on the trigger. There was a click.

There was a click, followed by a whirring noise; the film was rewinding. Scott pulled himself up from the floor and leaned against the sofa. He stared at the TV screen, his breath coming in harsh gasps.

"You still watching that garbage?" said his father. "Scaring yourself to death, as usual. You should be outside, Son, getting on with your own life—it's all before you."

The Slipscream

Ripples fanned, lazily slapping against the side of the boat. Jeremy peered into the water, but it was as dark as school gravy, and all he could make out was the point where the ripples met, arrowing toward him. Suddenly the waters parted and a tunnel edged with teeth thrust itself upward; jagged points gleamed in a scaly grinning mouth. Jeremy shrieked, clutching at his mother and shutting his eyes tight. He heard Bill laughing and suffered a hearty punch on the arm.

"Hey, Jerry, it's fake, it's not a real 'gator. Don't you know everything's fake in these places?"

He opened his eyes to find the other tourists staring at him from around the boat. One little girl, her gaping braces laced with strands of pink gum, was pointing at him.

"Mom, Mom, that big kid's scared!"

Bill put his arm around Jeremy's mother.

"See, Maureen, it's what I been saying all along. You protect the boy too much, it's made him soft. This is just what he needs—see a little of life, make a man of him."

Jeremy looked sulkily away to where the crocodile was attacking a python. He hated it when Bill touched his mother. In fact, he hated Bill.

"I want to be a real father to that boy," he'd said. "Give him a bang-up vacation, one he'll remember all his life, no expense spared. Florida, for instance." So here they were, in the tropical sun, theme parking. They'd seen everything from Disney World to Flea World, a universe populated by jolly bears and chipmunks and mice.

"That's all, folks," said the guide as the boat scraped along the pier. "Hope you enjoyed the trip. I enjoyed it so much I'm going to do it again . . . and again . . . and again."

The tourists tittered dutifully and filed out past the sweating line.

"Hold it!" cried Bill. He seized Jeremy's arm and pushed him against a pole with a metal flag on the top reading PICTURE POINT. "Smile, for God's sake." His fat legs set far apart, he bent over, fiddling behind the camera. "What's the matter with the boy, Maureen?"

"It's the heat. He's wilting."

"Not enough fresh air and exercise, that's your problem, Jerry. Look at you, pale as a snake's belly." He clicked the camera and gave it to Jeremy.

"Stand where I was, and the focus'll be just right. Here, Maureen." He clutched her to him as if she was a piece of luggage he mustn't lose, like the money pouch or the camera case. Unwillingly, Jeremy squinted through the viewfinder at them—his frail faded mother, smiling weakly

against a man swollen with confidence enough for two. BROOKLYN . . . ONLY THE STRONG SURVIVE, boasted his T-shirt. For Jeremy he'd bought a Garfield one that read LIFE IN THE SLOW LANE. Perched above his overripe face was a Mickey Mouse hat. Jeremy pretended the camera was a gun, aimed it, and carefully squeezed the trigger.

"Can I have a drink now?" he asked.

"What do you think, Bill?"

"One more ride, Jerry, one that'll get you nice and cool. Then you can have a Coke."

"How about this one?" He was looking wistfully at a flight of baby elephants circling the sky, gently rising and falling, their ears streaming behind them. They carried several infants and a group of Japanese businessmen.

"That's for babies, Jerry. I wouldn't be seen dead in a Dumbo, and I sincerely hope you wouldn't either. No, we're going to do the Haunted Mansion."

"Bill, he doesn't like the dark. It doesn't seem quite fair. . . . He's so imaginative."

"We'll put a stop to that then, won't we? You know I want only the best for little Jerry, and in my book that's not to be a whining wimp. This way."

Jeremy trudged along behind the stout red legs, watching the blue varicose veins snaking up the backs of Bill's knees into his Bermuda shorts. Higher up, parrots of all colors stretched painfully across his wide bottom. One of the worst things about standing in line, thought Jeremy, was the view. As they went into the Haunted Mansion, he clenched his fists, determined to give Bill no chance to tease him. It was, after all, a lot of silly nonsense, all faked; he knew that really. As long as he didn't let the dark get to him, he'd be all right.

The three of them, with Jeremy in the middle, climbed off the moving walkway and into the curved seat of the ghost train. As the safety bar smacked down, Jeremy felt a stab of panic.

"No smoking, eating or drinking, or flash photography," drawled a vampire as they rolled away into the dark. It wasn't too bad at first; ghouls' heads popping up and down, funny clocks and doors, and a creepy man with a dog. Jeremy could see they were made of wood or wax. It was when they got to the globe that he started to feel ill. There was a ghostly white head inside that was mouthing silently, and that, as well as being completely realistic, was transparent. His spine tingled; there was no way they could have faked that. The carts jerked away around a corner and began to slide downward. Surely it couldn't be the air-conditioning that was so cold, so dank? What was around the next bend? He had to get out of there.

"Shhhhhh Jeremy, for goodness' sake stop wiggling," hissed Bill.

They were gliding past a ballroom, looking down on it. Jeremy could feel his heart thudding so hard, he was sure Bill would feel it through their touching arms. He tried not to look, but from the corner of his eye he saw ghosts, real ones, haggard and gruesome, waltzing around and around in pairs. It must be over soon. Please, oh please, no more. If he kept his eyes shut, perhaps no one would notice.

The carts swiveled sharply sideways, and he heard Bill chuckling beside him. Despite himself, his eyes opened and he saw the worst horror of all. They were facing a great dark mirror, sailing past it. He could see the reflection of his mother on the left of the car, then his own pinched face; his white knuckles perched on the safety rail. But on the right—on the right, where Bill should have been, where the chuckling was coming from—was a skeleton.

He could still feel the soft damp fat of Bill's arm against

his, but in the mirror that flesh was melted away to strips of green decaying skin, thin as paper. There was a cobweb over one eye socket, where a spider hung from a thread. Those leering, chuckling tombstone teeth, where maggots squirmed, were close enough to touch.

The ride slid into the daylight. Jeremy stumbled over Maureen's feet and ran out into the bright heat. He leaned over a wall and heaved up his lunch into a bush. Too late he noticed a concealed speaker playing "Whistle While You Work."

"Well, that was fun, wasn't it?" said Bill. "Those holograms are so realistic! Got you going, didn't they Jerry, especially the one in the mirror? I swear your hair's standing on end. You look worse than anything back there."

"I think it's time to call it a day, Bill. Jeremy doesn't look all that well."

"Too many ice creams, eh? Tell you what, let's drive around a while, choose a restaurant."

This was Jeremy's favorite part of the day, sprawling in the back of the rented car, away from Bill's attention. As they cruised along the highway, they'd pass through landscapes so wild, dinosaurs might roam there, then all at once they'd turn down a boulevard lined with the totem poles of warring gods, winking neon against the sunset. . . . Pop-Eye's Famous Chicken 'n' Biscuit, Perkins Family Cake 'n' Steak, or Ploof's Pancakes. It was a land of plenty where people, cars, refrigerators were fat—even the grass was fat.

Jousting at King Henry's Castle flashed by, and The Elvis Museum—See Elvis's Reading Glasses. It was a far cry from a Sunday at home.

They pulled in finally at an Irish pub and were shown to a table by a waiter in Tyrolean shorts.

"Great!" said Bill.

"G'day!" said the waiter, unsure of the correct response. He handed out menus.

"Just a salad for this young man," said Bill. "He's been a little greedy. Myself, I think I'll have a large steak 'n' fries with all the trimmings, and Death by Chocolate to follow. And you, dear?"

"I'll have salad too," said Maureen, and then, "How do we all feel about a quiet day tomorrow? Maybe we've been overdoing it a little."

"We'll go swimming." Bill liked to be decisive. "I got my lifesaver's badge when I was Jerry's age. I suppose I could give him a few tips. Brush up your technique, eh?"

His salad arrived, and Jeremy's gloom was complete.

Dip 'n' Dive Waterworld actually looked like fun—Jeremy had to admit it. There were slides with tires, and slides with trays, and twisty, bouncy, ropy things. He couldn't wait to get into the water. Bill waddled out of the changing room, and Jeremy saw that while his hair was brown, the fuzz on his chest was white. Does Mom know he dyes his hair? he wondered maliciously.

"You go on in, Jerry," called Bill. "I'm just having a quick beer first." He sat down heavily at the bar, his stomach plumped up roundly on his thighs. There were white crescents under his breasts where the sun couldn't reach.

He's getting a little old, thought Jeremy, and he's tired. It came to him suddenly that Bill might be jealous of him.

"Dive in," shouted Maureen. "I'll take a picture!"

He surrendered to the joy of the water, testing his skills, moving from pool to pool. It was exhilarating. After an hour he swam back to the bar and found them still sitting there.

"Come on in, Mom. It's wonderful. I'll race you."

Bill pulled himself to his feet. "Time for our little lesson, I think. Did you know that swimming is the best possible exercise for the human body? Now look at your body. Not exactly a fine specimen, is it? Definitely a bit puny. So I'll show you the correct way to build it up."

This is war, thought Jeremy.

"All right," he answered amiably. "But first I want to go on the Slipscream. It's that water slide over there. The very high one. They say it's over a hundred feet tall, and the first half is free-fall. Are you coming?"

Bill hesitated.

"Oh, Bill," Maureen protested, "it's much too dangerous. Surely it's just for youngsters. . . ."

Bill pulled in his stomach, trying to pump it up into his chest and biceps. "You're as young as you feel, Maureen, and there's nothing this little ba— pipsqueak here can do that I can't. Lead the way, Jerry."

The slide looked even taller as they got nearer.

"It's about as tall as the hotel, wouldn't you say?" said Jeremy as they climbed the steps. Bill, for once, said nothing. Alternate stripes of sun and shadow slid monotonously over his fat back as their feet pounded onward and upward. He paused as they reached a sign reading UN-SUITABLE FOR PREGNANT WOMEN, OR THOSE SUFFERING FROM HEART CONDITIONS.

"You look like someone marching to the scaffold," re-marked Jeremy, and added, "Have you noticed that quite a lot of people come down again without daring to go on the slide?"

"Stop winding me up, Jerry," panted Bill, turning and pushing his face into Jeremy's. "Don't think I don't know what your game is. I've had quite enough from you this vacation, and I'm not going to put up with any more, do you understand? When we get back home, I'm going to marry your mother, and then we'll see who rules the roost. And it won't be you."

Jeremy wiped a fleck of spit from his cheek, and they started to walk up again. After a few steps he shouted, "I HATE it when you call me Jerry. My name's JEREMY!"

They arrived in a little hut at the top of the slide, where a lifeguard sat. The park was set out like a board game below them, complete with little Monopoly restau-rants and rest rooms. One of the swarming dots seemed to be wobbling.

"Mom's waving," said Jeremy, who had good eyesight. "She's going to take a picture."

Bill swallowed. "Um . . . What's the accident rate on this thing?" he asked the lifeguard.

"Oh, we haven't had an accident, well, not a bad one, for months. Go on, you'll enjoy it. Headfirst is real fun."

"After you, Jerry."

"JEREMY! No thanks. Too scary for me. You go, Bill."

The lifeguard encouraged him. "Remember to keep your legs and arms crossed, and whatever you do, DON'T sit up. You'll be just fine!"

Bill lay down on his back, his head sticking out over the sheer drop. His hands, folded across his chest, trembled slightly in his fuzzy white chest hair. His eyes were shut. He looked like the human sacrifice at the top of an Aztec temple. Water gushed from a thick pipe, gurgling past his body to shoot into the abyss. Behind them, on the steps, there was laughter and shouting. The guard leaned out of the back of the hut.

"Hey, what are you guys doing down there? Quit horsing around, or I'll call security."

"Ready?" said Jeremy. He put his hands on Bill's feet, about to push. Bill's eyes rolled open and widened, the pupils shrinking to dots as he stared defenselessly up at Jeremy. For an instant the same unthinkable thought occurred to them both. Then, as he began to slide over the edge, Bill's features convulsed in panic, and his belly concertinaed as he jerked upward.

The lifeguard turned back. "Watch it, you jerk!" he exclaimed, grabbing after Bill's ankles.

It was too late. Bill was spinning out into space, flailing into sunshine hot enough to burn the wings off Icarus, falling, twisting, bouncing off the plastic slide, getting smaller and smaller and smaller as he plunged toward the concrete. Jeremy thought he could just hear the *splat* of Bill landing. He leaned over for a better look. It was a little like when an insect flies into the windshield, he thought, and there were similar unpleasant smears across

the concrete. All the other little insects started scurrying around, and Jeremy turned away, shuddering. He rinsed his hands thoroughly, cleansing them of the touch of Bill's sweaty feet.

Through half-closed lids, Jeremy saw blurred green shapes through the window, which defined themselves into palm trees. He remembered where he was. Then he remembered what had happened yesterday and sat up in bed. It had been terrible—even Bill didn't deserve such a fate. Poor Mom was really upset too, but he would look after her. No one could look after her like he could. And today they would be going home again, to try and forget, and get on with life. Just the two of them, like it used to be.

He sprang quickly out of bed and ran into the shower. ". . . Scraped him off the pavement like a lump of strawberry jam," he found himself singing, to the tune of "John Brown's Body." "Glory, glory, what a helluva way to die . . ." and hastily changed it to a hum. To take his mind off things shocking and nasty, he pretended the shower was the cabinet of a mad scientist who had imprisoned him and was drilling holes in his body with laser beams.

"Bizzzzzzzz," he droned, turning up the hot water. He preferred his own fantasies to theme-park ones.

"Are you packed yet?" Maureen called. "There's a lot to do today. I have to make the arrangements to get the bod— to get Bill back home, and we've got to be at the airport by twelve." She was trying to be brave, to be practical. Jeremy got dressed and came out of the bathroom.

"Don't worry, Mom." He gave her a hug. "Everything's going to be fine. Let's go down to breakfast." They walked to the elevator, arm in arm, and Jeremy pressed the button. The doors slid open. He held them back for a maid with a cleaning cart, and they followed her in.

"Thank you kindly," she said. "You folks enjoying your vacation?"

"Yes, thanks," Jeremy said politely. Maureen was sniffling into a handkerchief. They turned to face the doors as they closed, and the elevator began to sink. There were mirrors all around it, and Jeremy could see his reflection, thin and pale in the dim light. He tried looking grief-stricken as practice for the funeral. After all, they were standing in a row like mourners at a graveside, with his mother on the left, her face buried in a hanky, while on his right . . . on his right—where he knew there was a maid with a brown-checked uniform and a cart with toilet paper and towels—he stared hard and blinked . . . on his right stood Bill. Large as life, wearing the shorts with the parrots, the money pouch, and the camera. It was a wonder he was standing at all; his bones looked as if they'd been rearranged, and a few of them stuck messily out of his skin. He was wearing the Mickey Mouse hat, for which Jeremy was grateful, because he could see a patch of brains, like oatmeal, oozing down the side of Bill's cheek. The skin was as red as ever, sagging in pouches over his T-shirt, but it had the chilly look of butcher's meat. The hands and ankles, Jeremy noticed, were beginning to turn purple. The lips parted glutinously in a grin, and an eye winked.

"You don't get rid of me that easily, Jerry," croaked the apparition. Before Jeremy could scream, the elevators bumped to the bottom. The vision faded, biding its time (for it had all the time in the world) as the maid jostled past with her cart.

"You have a nice day now!" she said.

About the Author/Illustrator

After she graduated from art school, Barbara Griffiths had an exhibition of her paintings at a prominent art gallery, which led to immediate and overwhelming success. She stopped her painting temporarily when she had her first child. Married with two children now, she has turned her talents to writing and illustrating books, combining an incredible imagination with appropriately haunting artwork. *Frankenstein's Hamster* is her first book.